ALL THROUGH THE NIGHT

Alvirah, lottery winner turned amateur sleuth, and her husband, Willy, are caught up in a Christmas mystery that calls on all of their skills and experience. Willy has been looking forward to playing Santa at the after-school centre recently set up to care for the children of working parents on New York's Upper West Side, and Alvirah has been busy with rehearsals for the Christmas pageant. But suddenly a shadow falls upon the Christmas cheer. The centre is threatened with closure, a deathbed will gives the promised replacement home to others, a valuable chalice, long missing, is spotted at the centre and disappears again, and a desperate young woman turns up, begging for Alvirah's help in finding the baby she abandoned seven years earlier. In a final blow, the young girl who is to play Mary in the Christmas pageant vanishes . . . A missing child. A stolen chalice. A desperate mother. Can Alvirah reach the truth in time for Christmas?

ALL THROUGH THE NIGHT

Mary Higgins Clark

CHIVERS PRESS
BATH

First published 1998
by
Simon & Schuster
This Large Print edition published by
Chivers Press
by arrangement with
Simon & Schuster UK Ltd
2000

ISBN 0 7540 1368 5

British Library Cataloguing in Publication Data available

Printed and bound in Great Britain by
REDWOOD BOOKS, Trowbridge, Wiltshire

ACKNOWLEDGEMENTS

When Michael Korda, my editor, called to suggest I write a Christmas story, my reply was, 'Michael, I am hanging up this phone.'

'Alvirah and Willy,' he said quickly, and I paused. Alvirah and Willy are my continuing characters. It's been a year since I wrote about them, and I've missed them.

All Through the Night is the result of that phone call. I hope you enjoy it. Love and thanks as always to Michael Korda for starting me on the path to telling it. Blessings to Michael and Senior Editor Chuck Adams for being my mentors, rooters, and coaches literally all through the night.

Grazie to Associate Director of Copy Editing Gypsy da Silva and to Carol Bowie; to agent Sam Pinkus, who researched the world of probate courts and family services for me; to my publicist Lisl Cade and daughter Carol Higgins Clark for their always prescient comments and suggestions; and last but surely not least to my husband, John Conheeney.

For John, with love,
and
For Bishop Paul G. Bootkoski, in loving
friendship.

CHAPTER ONE

Prologue

There were twenty-two days to go before Christmas, but Lenny was doing his Christmas shopping early this year. Secure in the knowledge that no one knew he was there, and standing so still and quiet that he hardly could hear himself breathe, he watched from the confessional as Monsignor Ferris went about the rounds of securing the church for the night. With a contemptuous smile, Lenny waited impatiently as the side doors were checked and the lights in the sanctuary extinguished. He shrank back when he saw the monsignor turn to walk down the side aisle, which meant that he would pass directly by the confessional. He cursed silently when a floorboard in the enclosure squeaked. Through a slit in the curtain he could see the clergyman stop and tilt his head, as if listening for another sound.

But then, as if satisfied, Monsignor Ferris resumed his journey to the back of the church. A moment later, the light in the vestibule was extinguished, and a door opened and closed. Lenny allowed himself an audible sigh—he was alone in St. Clement's church on West 103rd Street in Manhattan.

Sondra stood in the doorway of a townhouse across the street from the church. The building was under repair, and the temporary scaffolding around the street level shielded her from the view of passers-by. She wanted to be sure that Monsignor had left the church and was in the rectory before she left the baby. She had been attending services at St. Clement's for the last couple of days and had become familiar with his routine. She also knew that during Advent he would now be conducting a seven o'clock recitation of the rosary service.

Weak from the strain and fatigue of the birth only hours earlier, her breasts swelling with the fluid that preceded her milk, she leaned against the door frame for support. A faint whimper from beneath her partially buttoned coat made her arms move in the rocking motion instinctive to mothers.

On a plain sheet of paper that she would leave with the baby she had written everything she could safely reveal: 'Please give my little girl to a good and loving family to raise. Her father is of Italian descent; my grandparents were born in Ireland. Neither family has any hereditary diseases that I am aware of, so she should be healthy. I love her, but I cannot take care of her. If she asks about me someday,

2

show her this note, please. Tell her that the happiest hours of my life will always be the ones when I held her in my arms after she was born. For those moments it was just the two of us, alone in the world.'

Sondra felt her throat close as she spotted the tall, slightly stooped figure of the monsignor emerge from the church and walk directly to the adjacent rectory. It was time.

She had bought baby clothes and supplies, including a couple of shirts, a long nightgown, booties and a hooded jacket, bottles of formula and disposable diapers. She had wrapped the baby papoose-style, in two receiving blankets and a heavy woolen robe, but because the night was so cold, at the last minute she had brought along a brown paper shopping bag. She had read somewhere that paper was a good insulator against the cold. Not that the baby would be out in the frigid air for long, of course—just until Sondra could get to a phone and call the rectory.

She unbuttoned her coat slowly, shifting the baby only as needed, remembering to be especially careful of her head. The faint glow from the streetlight made it possible for her to see her infant's face clearly. 'I love you,' Sondra whispered fiercely. 'And I will *always* love you.' The baby stared up at her, her eyes fully open for the first time. Brown eyes stared into blue eyes, long dark-blond hair brushed against sprigs of the blond hair curling on the little forehead; tiny lips puckered and turned, seeking Mother's breast.

Sondra pressed the baby's head against her neck; her lips lingered on the soft cheek; her hand caressed the infant's back and legs. Then, in a decisive move, she slipped the tiny figure into the shopping bag, reached for the secondhand stroller folded next to her and tucked the handle under one arm.

She waited until several people had walked past her hiding place, then hurried to the curb and looked up and down the street. A block away traffic was stopped at the red light, but she saw no pedestrians coming in either direction.

A solid wall of parked cars on both sides of the street helped to protect Sondra from any curious eyes as she darted across the street to the rectory. There she ran up the three steps to the narrow stoop and opened the stroller. After engaging the brake, she laid the baby snugly under the stroller's hood and laid the bundle of clothes and bottles at her feet. She knelt for a moment and took one last look at her child. 'Good-bye,' she whispered. Then she stood and quickly ran down the steps and headed toward Columbus Avenue.

She would make the call to the rectory from a street phone two blocks away.

Lenny prided himself on being in and out of a
church in less than three minutes. You never
know about silent alarms, he thought, as he
opened his backpack and pulled out a
flashlight. Keeping the narrow beam pointed
toward the floor, he quickly began to make his
usual rounds. He went to the poor box first.
Donations had been down lately, he'd noticed,
but this one yielded a better than usual take,
somewhere between thirty and forty dollars.

The offering boxes below the votive candles
turned out to be the most satisfactory of any of
the last ten churches he had hit. There were
seven of them, placed at intervals in front of
the statues of the saints. Quickly he smashed
the locks and grabbed the cash.

In the last month he'd come to Mass here a
couple of times to study the layout; he had
observed that the priest consecrated the bread
and wine in plain goblets, so he didn't bother
to break into the tabernacle, since there'd be
nothing special there. He was just as glad to
avoid doing that anyway. The couple of years
he'd spent in parochial school had had an
effect on him, he acknowledged, making him
queasy about doing certain things. It definitely
got in his way when it came to robbing
churches.

On the other hand, he had no qualms about

5

leaving with the prize that had brought him here in the first place, the silver chalice with the star-shaped diamond at the base. It had belonged to Joseph Santori, the priest who founded St. Clement's parish one hundred years ago, and it was the one treasure this historic church contained.

A painting of Santori hung above a mahogany cabinet in a recess to the right of the sanctuary. The cabinet was ornate, its grillwork designed to both protect and display the chalice. After one of the masses he had attended, Lenny had drifted over to read the plaque beneath the cabinet.

At his ordination in Rome, Father, later Bishop, Santori was given this cup by Countess Maria Tomicelli. It had been in her family since the days of early Christianity. At age 45, Joseph Santori was consecrated as a bishop and assigned to the See of Rochester. Upon his retirement at age 75, he returned to St. Clement's, where he spent his remaining years working among the poor and the elderly. Bishop Joseph Santori's reputation for holiness was so widespread that after his death, a petition was signed to ask the Holy See to consider him for beatification, a cause that remains active today.

The diamond definitely would bring a few bucks, Lenny thought as he swung his hatchet. With two hard blows he smashed the hinges of the cabinet. He yanked open the doors and grabbed the chalice. Afraid that he might have triggered a silent alarm, he quickly ran to the side door of the church, unlocked it and pushed it open, anxious now to get out.

As he turned west toward Columbus Avenue, the cold air quickly dried the perspiration that had covered his face and back. Once on the avenue, he knew he could disappear into the crowds of shoppers. But as he passed the rectory, the wail of an approaching police siren shattered the calm.

He could see two couples down the block, headed in the same direction he was going, but he didn't dare to start running to catch up with them. That would be a sure giveaway. Then he spotted the stroller on the rectory steps. In an instant he was carrying it down to the sidewalk. There appeared to be nothing in it but a couple of shopping bags. Shoving his backpack in the foot of the stroller, he walked quickly to catch up with the couples ahead of him. Once he was near them, he strolled sedately just behind.

The police car roared past the group and screeched to a halt in front of the church. At Columbus Avenue, Lenny quickened his steps, no longer worried about detection. On such a chilly night, all pedestrians were hurrying, anxious to reach their destinations. He would just blend in. There was no reason for anyone to pay attention to the average-sized, sharp-faced man in his early thirties, who was wearing a cap and a plain, dark jacket and pushing a cheap, well-worn stroller.

*　　　*　　　*

The street phone Sondra had planned to call from was in use. Wildly anxious with impatience and already heartsick about the baby she had abandoned, she tried to decide whether to interrupt the caller, a man wearing the uniform of a security guard. She could explain that it was an emergency.

I can't do that, she thought despairingly. Tomorrow, if there's a story in the newspapers about the baby, he might remember me and talk to the police. Dismayed, she shoved her hands in her pockets, groping for the coins she needed and the paper on which she'd written the phone number of the rectory, unnecessary because she knew it by heart.

It was December 3rd, and already Christmas lights and decorations glittered from the windows of the shops and restaurants along Columbus Avenue. A couple walking hand in hand passed Sondra, their faces radiant as they smiled at each other. The girl appeared to be

8

about eighteen, her own age, Sondra thought, although she felt infinitely older—and infinitely removed from the air of careless joy this couple displayed.

It was getting colder. Was the baby wrapped warmly enough? she worried. For an instant she shut her eyes. O, God, please make this man get off the phone, she prayed, I need to make this call now.

An instant later she heard the click of the receiver being replaced. Sondra waited until the caller was a few paces away before she grabbed the receiver, dropped in the coins and dialed.

'St. Clement's rectory.' The voice was that of an elderly man. It had to be the old priest she had seen at Mass.

'Please, may I speak to Monsignor Ferris, right away.'

'I'm Father Dailey. Perhaps I can help you. Monsignor is outside with the police. We have an emergency.'

'Quietly, Sondra broke the connection. They had found the baby already. She was safe now, and Monsignor Ferris would see that she was placed in a good home.

An hour later Sondra was on the bus to Birmingham, Alabama, where she was a student in the music department of the university, a violin student whose astonishing talent had already marked her for future stardom on the concert stage.

*   *   *

It was not until he was in the apartment of his elderly aunt that Lenny heard the faint mewling of the infant.

Startled, he looked into the stroller. He saw the shopping bag begin to move and quickly tore it open; he stared in shock at the tiny occupant. Unbelieving, he unpinned the note from the blanket, read it and mouthed an expletive.

From the bedroom at the end of the narrow hallway, his aunt called: 'Is that you, Lenny?' There was no hint of a welcome in the greeting, spoken with a strong accent that betrayed her Italian roots.

'Yes, Aunt Lilly.' There was no way he could simply hide the baby. He had to figure out what to do. What should he tell her?

Lilly Maldonado walked down the hall to the living room. At seventy-four, she both looked and moved like someone ten years younger than her age. Her hair, pulled back in a tight bun, was still generously sprinkled with black strands; her brown eyes were large and lively, and her short, ample body moved in quick, sure steps.

Along with Lenny's mother, her younger sister, she had emigrated to the United States from Italy shortly after World War II. A skilled seamstress, she had married a tailor from her native village in Tuscany and worked side by side with him in their tiny Upper West Side shop until his death five years ago. Now she worked out of her apartment, or went to the homes of her devoted clients, whom she charged far too little for dressmaking and alterations.

But as her customers joked among themselves, in exchange for Lilly's low prices, they were forced to lend considerable sympathetic attention to her endless stories about her troublesome nephew Lenny.

On her knees, a heap of pins beside her, her alert eyes carefully measuring as she chalked hem lengths, Lilly would sigh, then launch into her litany of complaints. 'My nephew. He's always driving me crazy. Trouble from the day he was born. When he was in school: Don't ask. Arrested. Went away to a prison for kids twice. Did that straighten him out? No. Never can hold a job. Why not? My sister, his mama, God rest her, always was too easy on him. I love him, of course—after all, he's my flesh and blood—but he drives me crazy. How much can I put up with, him coming in at all hours? What's he *living* on, I ask you?'

But now, after earnest prayer to her beloved St. Francis of Assisi, Lilly Maldonado had made a decision. She had tried everything, and none of it had made a difference. Clearly nothing was going to change Lenny, and so she was going to wash her hands of him once and for all.

The light in the foyer was dim, and she was so intent on delivering her speech that she did not immediately notice the stroller behind him.

Her arms folded, her voice firm, Lilly said, 'Lenny, you asked if you could stay a few nights. Well, that was three weeks ago, and I don't want you here anymore. Pack your bags and get out.'

Lilly's loud, strident tone startled the already stirring infant, and the faint mewling broke into a wail.

'What?' Lilly exclaimed. Then she saw the stroller. In a quick move, she shoved her nephew aside and looked down into it. Shocked, she snapped, 'What have you done now? Where did you get that baby?'

Lenny thought fast. He didn't want to leave this apartment. It was a perfect place to live, and staying with his aunt gave him the aura of respectability. He had read the note from the baby's mother, so he quickly came up with a plan.

'She's mine, Aunt Lilly. A girl I was crazy about is the mother. But she's moving to California and wants to put the baby up for adoption. I don't want to. I want to keep her.'

The wail was now a demanding screech. Tiny fists flailed the air.

Lilly opened the bundle at the infant's feet. 'The baby's hungry,' she announced. 'At least your girlfriend sent some formula.' She plucked out one of the bottles and thrust it at Lenny. 'Here, warm this up.'

Her expression changed as she unwrapped the blankets from around the tiny infant, picked her up and cradled her in warm and comforting arms. 'Beautiful, *bella*. How could your mama not want you?' She looked at Lenny. 'What do you call her?'

Lenny thought of the star-shaped diamond in the chalice. 'Her name is Star, Aunt Lilly.'

'Star,' Lilly Maldonado murmured as she soothed the sobbing baby. 'In Italy we would call her Stellina. That means "little star." '

Through narrowed eyes, Lenny watched the bonding between the infant and the aging woman. No one would be looking for the baby, he thought. It wasn't like he had kidnapped it, and anyhow, if anything ever *did* come up about the kid, he'd have the note to prove she had been abandoned., He knew the word for grandmother in Italian was *nonna*. As he turned and hurried into the kitchen to warm the bottle, Lenny told himself with satisfaction, 'Star, my little girl, I've found me a home— and you've got yourself a *nonna*.'

CHAPTER TWO

Seven Years Later

Frowning, Willy Meehan sat at the piano his wife, Alvirah, had bought him for his sixty-second birthday. With intense concentration, he attempted to read the notes in the *John Thompson's Book for Mature Beginners*. Maybe it will be easier if I sing along, he thought. 'Sleep, my child, and peace attend thee,' he began.

Willy has such a good voice, Alvirah thought, as she came into the room. 'All Through the Night' is one of my favorite carols, she reflected, as she looked affectionately at her husband of more than forty years. In profile, his resemblance to the late Tip O'Neill, the legendary Speaker of the House of Representatives, was even more startling than when viewed full on, she decided. With his shock of white hair, his craggy features, his keen blue eyes and warm smile, Willy was often the recipient of startled glances of recognition, even though it was several years since O'Neill's passing.

Now, to her loving eyes, he looked simply splendid in the dark blue suit he'd worn out of respect for Bessie Durkin Maher, whose wake they were about to attend. Alvirah had

15

reluctantly switched from the size twelve navy suit she'd been planning to wear to a black dress that was a size larger. She and Willy had just returned the previous evening from their post-Thanksgiving cruise in the Caribbean, and the sumptuous food had dealt a mortal blow to her diet.

'Guardian angels God will send thee,' Willy sang as he played.

The dear Lord God sure did send his angels to us, Alvirah thought as—not wanting to disturb Willy—she tiptoed to the window to enjoy the breathtaking view of Central Park.

Only a little over two years ago Alvirah, then a cleaning woman, and Willy, a plumber, had been living in Jackson Heights in Queens, in the apartment they had rented long ago as newlyweds. She had been bone weary after a particularly hard day at Mrs. O'Keefe's, who always felt that she didn't get her money's worth unless Alvirah moved every stick of furniture in the house when she vacuumed. Still, as they did every Wednesday and Saturday evening, they had paused to watch television when the lottery numbers were announced as the balls popped into place. They'd almost had a collective heart attack when one after another, their numbers, the ones they always played, came up.

And then we realized we'd won forty million dollars, Alvirah thought, still incredulous at

16

their good luck.

We weren't just *lucky*, though, we were blessed, she corrected herself, as she drank in the view. It was quarter of seven, and Central Park was softly beautiful with fresh snow that had left a shimmering white coverlet on the trees and fields. In the distance, festive Christmas lights illuminated the area surrounding the Tavern on the Green. The headlights of cars and taxis were a moving river of brightness as they wound their way along the curving roads. Anywhere else they would just look like traffic, she mused. The horse-drawn carriages, not visible to her now, but no doubt present in the park, always reminded her of the stories her mother told about growing up near Central Park in the early part of the century. Likewise the skaters waltzing on the Wollman Rink ice reminded her of evenings years ago when she had roller-skated to organ music at St. Raymond's in the Bronx.

After winning the lottery, with its yearly income of two million dollars, minus taxes, she and Willy had moved to this luxurious apartment. Living on Central Park always had been one of her fantasies, and besides, the apartment was a good investment. However, they still kept their old rental apartment in Jackson Heights, just in case New York State went broke and quit paying them.

17

Truthfully, though, Alvirah had made good use of her newfound wealth, giving quite a lot to charity while managing to enjoy herself immensely. Plus she'd had some memorable experiences. She had gone to Cypress Point Spa in Pebble Beach and almost got murdered there because of her nose for news. The experience paid off when she became a contributing columnist for the *New York Globe*, and, as one thing always leads to another, with the aid of the recording device in her sunburst lapel pin, she had solved a number of crimes, gradually earning herself a reputation as a real sleuth, though still an amateur, to be sure.

Willy's skills as a plumber were now utilized exclusively by his oldest sibling, Sister Cordelia, who tended to the poor and elderly on the Upper West Side of Manhattan. She kept Willy busy repairing sinks and toilets and heating units in the tenements of her charges.

Before they left on the cruise, he had worked double time fixing up the second floor of the abandoned furniture store where Cordelia ran a clothing thrift shop. Called Home Base, it was also an unofficial after-school center for young children, from the first to the fifth grade, whose parents were working.

Yes, Alvirah had decided, having money was a fine thing, so long as one never forgot how to live without it, something she and Willy intended never to do. It's nice that we can help out other people, she thought, but if we were to lose every dime of the money, we'd be happy as long as we're together.

'*All through the night,*' Willy concluded with a decisive crescendo. 'Ready to go, hon?' he asked as he pushed back the piano bench.

'All set,' Alvirah said as she turned to face him. 'You sounded just great. You play with so much feeling. So many people just rush through these sweet songs.'

Willy smiled benevolently. While he heartily regretted the moment he had casually mentioned to Alvirah that he wished he had taken piano lessons as a child, he realized that he was beginning to derive intense satisfaction whenever he managed to play through a song without a single mistake.

'The reason I played so slowly was because I couldn't read the notes any faster,' he joked. 'Anyhow, we'd better get going.'

*   *   *

The funeral home was on Ninety-sixth Street, just off Riverside Drive. As their cab made its laborious way uptown, Alvirah reflected on her friends Bessie and Kate Durkin. She had known Bessie and Kate for many years. Kate had worked as a salesperson in Macy's, and Bessie had been the live-in housekeeper for a retired judge and his ailing wife.

19

When the judge's wife died, Bessie had handed in her resignation, saying she could not possibly stay under the same roof with the judge without the presence of another woman.

A week later, Judge Aloysius Maher had requested her hand in marriage, and so, after sixty years of maidenhood, Bessie promptly accepted the offer. Once married, she had settled in to make his large and handsome townhouse on the Upper West Side her own.

After over forty years of marriage, and a blessedly happy one at that, Willy and Alvirah had reached the point where they typically thought about the same subject even before they discussed it. 'Bessie knew just what she was doing when she quit her job,' Willy commented, his words melding seamlessly with Alvirah's own unspoken thought. 'She knew if she didn't grab the judge before other women got their hooks into him, she didn't stand a chance. She always treated that house as if she owned it, and it would have killed her to be booted out of it.'

'True, she loved it all right,' Alvirah agreed. 'And to be fair, she kept her part of the bargain. She was a marvelous housekeeper and could cook like an angel. The judge couldn't get to the table fast enough. You have to admit she waited on him hand and foot.'

Willy had never been a fan of Bessie Durkin's. 'She knew what she was doing. The judge only lasted eight years. Then Bessie got the house *and* a pension, invited Kate to move in, and Kate's waited on *her* hand and foot ever since.'

'Kate's a saint,' Alvirah said in agreement, 'but of course the house will be hers now that Bessie's gone, and she'll have an income. She should be able to manage just fine.'

Cheered by her own optimistic statement, she glanced out the window. 'Oh, Willy, don't you love the Christmas decorations in all the windows?' she asked. 'It's such a shame Bessie died so near the holidays; she always loved them so.'

'It's only the fourth of December,' Willy pointed out. 'She made it through Thanksgiving.'

'That's true,' Alvirah conceded. 'I'm glad we were with them. Remember how much she enjoyed her turkey? She ate every bite of it.'

'And everything else in sight,' Willy said dryly. 'Here we are.'

As their taxi pulled up to the curb, an attendant at the Reading Funeral Home opened the door for them and, in a subdued tone, told them that Bessic Durkin Maher was reposing in the east parlor. The heavy, sweet smell of flowers drifted through the hushed atmosphere as they walked sedately down the corridor.

'These places give me the creeps,' Willy

21

commented. 'They always smell of dead carnations.'

In the east parlor they joined a group of some thirty mourners, including Vic and Linda Baker, the couple who had rented the top floor apartment of Bessie's townhouse. They were standing at the head of the casket next to Bessie's sister Kate, and, like family, were accepting condolences with her.

'What's *that* all about?' Willy whispered to Alvirah as they waited their turn to speak to Kate.

Thirteen years younger than her formidable sister, Kate was a wiry seventy-five-year-old with a cap of short gray hair and warm blue eyes that were now welling with tears.

She's been bullied all her life by Bessie, Alvirah thought, as she enveloped Kate in her arms. 'It's for the best, Kate,' she said firmly. 'If Bessie had survived that stroke she'd have been a total invalid, and that wasn't for her.'

'No,' Kate agreed, brushing away a tear. 'She wouldn't have wanted that. I guess I've always thought of Bessie as both my sister *and* my mother. She might have been set in her ways, but she had a good heart.'

'We'll miss her terribly,' Alvirah said, as behind her Willy breathed a deep sigh.

As Willy gave Kate a brotherly hug, Alvirah turned to Vic Baker. So formal was his mourning attire that Alvirah immediately was

22

reminded of one of the Addams Family characters. Baker, a stocky man in his mid-thirties, with a boyish face, dark brown hair and shrewd china-blue eyes, was wearing a black suit with a black tie. Beside him, his wife, Linda, also dressed in black, was holding a handkerchief to her face.

Trying to squeeze out a tear no doubt, Alvirah thought dryly. She had met Vic and Linda for the first time on Thanksgiving. Aware of her sister's failing health, Kate had invited Alvirah and Willy, Sister Cordelia, Sister Maeve Marie and Monsignor Thomas Ferris, the pastor of St. Clement's who resided in the rectory a few doors from Bessie's townhouse on West 103rd Street, to share the holiday dinner with them.

Vic and Linda had stopped in as they were having coffee, and it seemed to Alvirah that Kate had pointedly not invited them to stay for dessert. So what were they doing acting like the chief mourners? Alvirah asked herself as she dismissed Linda's apparent sadness, assuming it to be phony.

A lot of people would think she's good-looking, Alvirah conceded as she took in Linda's even features, but I'd hate to get on the wrong side of her. There's a coldness to her eyes that I don't trust, and that spiky hairdo with all those brassy gold highlights is the pits.

'. . . as though she were my own mother,' Linda was saying, a quiver in her voice.

Willy, of course, had heard the remark and couldn't help adding his own. 'You rented that apartment less than a year ago, didn't you?' he asked.

Without waiting for an answer, he took Alvirah's arm and propelled her toward the kneeling bench.

In death as in life, Bessie Durkin looked to be in charge of the situation. Attired in her best print dress, wearing the narrow strand of faux pearls the judge had given her on their wedding day, her hair styled and combed, Bessie had the satisfied expression of someone who had successfully made a lifelong habit of getting other people to do things her way.

Later, when Alvirah and Willy were leaving, they said good-bye to Kate, promising to he at the funeral Mass at St. Clement's and ride in the car with her to the cemetery. 'Sister Cordelia is coming too,' Kate told them. 'Willy, I've been worried about her this week that you've been away. She's been under so much strain. The city inspectors are giving her a terrible time about Home Base.'

'We expected as much,' Willy said. I called today, but she was out and didn't get back to me. I had expected to see her here tonight.'

Glancing across the room, Kate saw Linda Baker bearing down on them. She dropped her

24

voice. 'I asked Sister back to the house after the funeral,' she whispered. I want you to come too, and Monsignor will be there.'

They said their good-nights, and because Willy said he had to get some fresh air just to get the overwhelming smell of flowers off him, they agreed to walk a ways before hailing a taxi.

'Did you notice how Linda Baker came running when she saw us talking to Kate?' Alvirah asked Willy as they strolled arm in arm toward Columbus Avenue.

'I sure did. I have to say there was something about that woman that bothered me. And now I'm worried about Cordelia too. She's no spring chicken, and I think she's bitten off more than she can chew by trying to mind those kids after school.'

'Willy, they're just being kept warm and safe until their mothers can pick them up from work. How can anyone find fault with that?'

'The city can. Like it or not, there are rules and regulations about minding kids. Hold on, I've had enough of this cold air. Here comes a cab.'

CHAPTER THREE

'Like it or not, there are rules and regulations,' Sister Cordelia said with a sigh, as she unconsciously repeated Willy's exact words the next day. 'They've given me a deadline— January 1st—and Inspector Pablo Torres told me he was already breaking every rule in the book to stretch it that far.'

It was one o'clock, and after a Mass of Resurrection, Bessie Durkin had been lowered into her final resting place, alongside three generations of Durkins in Calvary Cemetery.

Willy and Alvirah, Sister Cordelia and her assistant, Sister Maeve Marie, who was a twenty-nine-year-old former NYPD policewoman, and Monsignor Thomas Ferris were at the table in Bessie's townhouse, enjoying the Virginia ham, homemade potato salad and sourdough biscuits prepared by Kate.

'Is there anything else I can get anyone?' Kate asked meekly before she took her place at the table.

'Kate, sit down,' Alvirah ordered. She turned to Cordelia. 'What are the specific problems that are so terrible, Cordelia?' she asked.

For a moment the troubled frown on the face of the seventy-year-old nun disappeared.

27

Cordelia's eyes softened as she looked at her sister-in-law and smiled. 'It's nothing even you can fix, Alvirah. We have thirty-six kids, ages six to eleven, who come to us after school. I asked Pablo if he'd rather have them on the streets. I asked him what we're doing wrong. We give them a snack. We've rounded up some trustworthy high school kids who help them with their homework and play games with them. There are always adult volunteers in the thrift shop, so there's plenty of supervision at all times. The kids' mothers or fathers pick them up by six-thirty. We don't charge anything, of course. The nurses at the schools have checked any kids we take in. They've never complained about anything.'

Cordelia sighed and shook her head.

'We know the property is in the process of being sold,' Sister Maeve explained, 'but it's at least a year before we have to get out. We've freshly spackled and painted the whole second floor where the kids stay when they're there, so there isn't a peeling chip anywhere. Apparently it's still a problem though, because they say that lead paint was used years ago. Sister Superior asked Pablo if he'd taken a look at some of the places where these kids live and compared the conditions there to those at Home Base. He said he doesn't make the rules. He said there have to be two exits, and they can't include the fire escape.'

28

'The staircase is wide enough for five kids to come down together, but they don't count that. Maeve, we could go on and on,' Sister Cordelia interrupted. 'The bottom line is that in under four weeks we have to close the doors on the Home Base program, and if any of those kids show up, we have no choice but to send them home to an empty apartment with no security and no supervision.'

Monsignor Ferris reached for his empty cup as Kate held up the teapot. 'Thank you, yes, Kate. And I think it's time to share our good news with the others.'

Kate looked shy. 'Why don't you, please, Monsignor?'

'Gladly. Bessie, God rest her, realized the end was near, and the day after Thanksgiving she asked me to stop in.'

Let this news be what I think it is, Alvirah prayed silently.

The quiet composure that was a habitual expression on Monsignor Ferris's kindly face was brightened by the obviously happy tidings he was about to impart. He smoothed his silver hair, which still was somewhat disheveled from the wind at the graveside service, then he smiled. 'Bessie told me that, of course, in her will she left this house to her sister, as well as an income that would ensure Kate's comfort, but Kate had indicated to her that she would like to turn the house over to Sister Cordelia

29

for the Home Base program.'

'Saints preserve us!' Cordelia said fervently. 'Oh, Kate.'

'Kate would want to stay on, living in the fourth floor apartment the Bakers are now occupying. Bessie quite frankly wasn't enthusiastic about the idea, but felt it was Kate's decision to make, and she asked me to make sure nothing went wrong with all the arrangements.'

'You know Bessie always treated me as if I couldn't find my own way to the store,' Kate said fondly.

'I told Bessie that with the rectory just three doors down, there'd be no problem keeping an eye on everything, although I also told her that Kate is very much able to handle her own affairs,' the monsignor explained.

'I'll love having Home Base here,' Kate said. 'I've wanted to volunteer to help ever since you opened it, Cordelia, but Bessie needed me.'

Monsignor Ferris stood, smiling as he watched the news register on Sister Cordelia's face. 'I've always believed foresight should be considered a cardinal virtue,' he announced. 'I happen to have a bottle of champagne cooling in the ice bucket. I think a toast to the Durkin sisters, Bessie and Kate, is in order.'

This is such wonderful news. So why am I so worried? Alvirah asked herself. Why am I sure that something is going to go wrong? Mentally

30

she examined the possibilities in much the same way she might use her tongue to seek out the source of a toothache. It only took an instant to find the source of her concern: the Bakers.

'Are you sure you can get the Bakers out, Kate?' she asked. It isn't so easy to get rid of tenants these days.'

'Absolutely sure,' Kate said firmly. 'The lease is for one year, and it's up in January. There is a specific clause saying that the renewal is solely at the discretion of the owner. You remember how we had that young man in that apartment who was an exercise nut? At least once a week he'd drop a barbell, and always in the middle of the night. Bessie was sure the house would cave in. You know how she loved this place. After she finally got rid of him, she added the renewal clause to the lease for the new tenants.'

'Looks as though you've thought of everything,' Willy observed.

'I do feel sorry about telling them they have to move, but I'll be honest—I'll be glad when they're gone,' Kate said. 'Vic Baker is always underfoot, looking for things to fix around here. You'd think he *owned* the house.'

*   *   *

When they left an hour later, Willy and

Alvirah walked Monsignor Ferris to the door of the rectory. The already cloudy sky was now completely overcast. The wind had become sharp, and the raw, damp cold was bone penetrating.

'They're predicting a long winter,' Alvirah said. 'Can you imagine in a couple of weeks, having to tell those little kids that they can't go to Home Base, where they're safe and warm and comfortable?'

It was a rhetorical question, of course, and as she asked it, even Alvirah was only half listening. Instead, her attention was directed across the street, where a young woman in a sweat suit was standing, staring at the rectory.

'Monsignor Tom,' she said. 'See that woman. Don't you think there's something odd about the way she's just standing there?'

He nodded. 'I saw her there yesterday, and then she was at early Mass this morning. I caught up to her before she left and asked if I could help her in any way. She just shook her head and almost rushed away. If she has a problem she wants to discuss, I think I'm going to have to let her come to me.'

Willy put a restraining hand on Alvirah's arm. 'Don't forget we're due at Home Base to help Cordelia with the rehearsal for the Christmas pageant,' he reminded her.

'Meaning mind my own business. Well, I suppose you're right,' Alvirah agreed cheerfully.

She glanced across the street again. The young woman was walking rapidly away, headed west. Alvirah squinted to get a good look at her classic profile even as she admired her regal carriage. 'She looks familiar,' she said flatly. 'I'll have to put on my thinking cap.'

CHAPTER FOUR

They're talking about me, Sondra thought as she hurried away. The townhouse she had been standing in front of was no longer under repair, as it had been before. There was no scaffolding to shield her today as she tried to decide what to do.

But what *could* she do? Certainly she couldn't buy back that moment seven years ago when she had crossed the street, opened the stroller and left her baby on the rectory stoop. If only. If only, she thought. Then: Dear God, where can I turn? What happened to her? Who took my little girl? She fought back tears.

A cab with its light on was stopped in traffic. She raised her hand to signal the driver. 'The Wyndham, on West Fifty-eighth between Fifth and Sixth,' she said as she got into the backseat.

'First visit to New York?' the cabbie asked.

'No.' But I haven't been here in seven years, she thought. Her first visit had been when she was twelve and her grandfather brought her here from Chicago to a Midori concert at Carnegie Hall. He had brought her twice again after that. 'Someday you will play on that stage,' he had promised her solemnly. 'You have the gift. You can be as successful as she.'

A violinist whose hands had been limited by arthritis, cutting short his career, her grandfather had made his living as a music teacher and critic. And supported me, Sondra thought sadly—when he was sixty years old he took me in.

She had been only ten when her young parents had been killed in an accident. Granddad devoted himself to me, taught me everything he knew about music, she reminded herself. And he used every spare penny he could find to take me to hear the great violinists.

Her talent had earned her a full scholarship to the University of Birmingham, and it was there, in the spring of her freshman year, that she met Anthony del Torre, a pianist visiting the campus for a concert. What followed should never have happened.

How could I have told Granddad that I got involved with a man I knew was married? she asked herself now. *I couldn't have kept the baby. There was no money to pay for help. I had years of schooling ahead of me. And if I had told him what had happened, it would have broken his heart.*

As the cab made its way through the slow traffic, Sondra thought back to that wrenching time. She thought about how she had saved money to come to New York, she remembered checking into a cheap hotel on November

36

30th, buying the baby clothes and diapers, the bottles and formula and stroller. She had located the hospital, closest to the hotel and had planned to go to the emergency room when she went into labor. She would, of course, have to give a false name and address. But the baby had come so quickly on December 3rd; there had been no time to get to the hospital.

Early in the pregnancy, she had decided that New York was where she would leave the baby. She loved the city. From her very first visit there with her granddad, she knew that someday she would live in Manhattan. She had instantly felt at home there. On that first visit, her grandfather had taken her to St. Clement's, the church he had attended throughout his boyhood. 'Whenever I wanted a special favor, I would kneel in the pew nearest Bishop Santori's picture and his chalice,' he told her. 'From them I always received comfort. Sondra, I went there when I realized there was no hope for the stiffening fingers. That was the nearest I ever came to despair.'

In the several days before the baby was born, Sondra had slipped in and out of St. Clement's; each time she had knelt in that pew. She had watched the clergymen there; she'd seen the kindness in the face of Monsignor Ferris and knew that she could

37

trust him to find a good home for her baby.

Where is my baby now? Sondra wondered in despair.

She'd been in agony since yesterday. As soon as she checked into the hotel, she had phoned the rectory and said she was a reporter following up on the story of the baby who had been left on the stoop of the rectory on December 3rd, seven years ago.

The astonishment in the secretary's voice had warned her of what was to come. '*A baby left at St. Clement's?!* I'm afraid you're wrong. I've been here twenty years, and nothing like that has ever happened.'

The cab turned onto Central Park South. I used to daydream that maybe the people who adopted the baby were pushing her in her carriage here, along the park, Sondra thought, where the baby could see the horses and carriages.

Late yesterday afternoon she had gone to the public library and called up the microfilm of the New York newspapers of December 4th, seven years ago. The only reference to St. Clement's that day was an article about a theft there, stating that the chalice of Bishop Santori, the founding pastor to whom many of the devout prayed, had been stolen.

That's probably why the police were there when I called that night; that's why the monsignor was outside, Sondra thought, her distress growing. And I believed it was because they'd found the baby.

Then who *had* taken the baby? She had left her in a paper shopping bag for added warmth. Maybe some kids had come by and pushed the stroller away and abandoned it, without ever realizing she was there. Suppose the baby had died of exposure.

I'd go to prison, Sondra thought. What would that do to Granddad? He keeps telling me that all the sacrifices he's made over the years have been worthwhile because of what I've become. He's so proud that I'll be playing a concert at Carnegie Hall on December 23rd. It's what he always dreamed of—first for himself, and then for me.

The celebrity-studded charity affair would introduce her to the New York critics. Yo-Yo Ma, Plácido Domingo, Kathleen Battle, Emanuel Ax and the brilliant young violinist Sondra Lewis were the main attractions. She still could hardly believe it.

'We're here, miss,' the cabbie said, an edge in his voice. With a start, Sondra realized that his irritation was due to the fact that he'd already told her that once.

'Oh, sorry.' The fare was $3.40. She fished in her wallet for a five-dollar bill. 'That's fine,' she said, opening the door and starting to get out.

'I don't think you really wanted to give me a

forty-five dollar tip, miss.'

Sondra looked at the fifty-dollar bill the cabbie was holding out to her. 'Oh, thank you,' she stammered.

'That's a big mistake, lady. Lucky for you I don't take advantage of pretty young women.'

As Sondra exchanged the fifty for a five-dollar bill, she thought—too bad you weren't around when I traded my baby for my grandfather's good opinion of me and my own chance at success.

CHAPTER FIVE

When they reached the building on Amsterdam Avenue—formerly the Goldsmith and Son Furniture Emporium—that now housed Sister Cordelia's clothing thrift shop, Alvirah and Willy went directly to the second floor.

It was four o'clock, and the children who regularly came to Home Base to take advantage of the after-school facilities were sitting cross-legged on the floor around Sister Maeve Marie. The large area had been transformed into a kind of bright and cheery auditorium. The faded linoleum was polished to the point that even the floorboards beneath the worn spaces glistened.

The walls were painted sunshine yellow and decorated with drawings and cutouts the children had made. Old-fashioned radiators whistled and thudded, but thanks to Willy and his near-magical ability to fix the unfixable, there was no mistaking the warmth they provided.

'Today is very special,' Sister Maeve Marie was saying. 'We're going to begin practice for our Christmas pageant.'

Willy and Alvirah slipped into seats near the staircase and watched affectionately. A regular volunteer at Home Base, Alvirah was in

41

charge of the party that was to follow the pageant, and Willy would be playing Santa Claus.

The children's expectant and lively eyes were riveted on Sister Maeve Marie as she explained, 'Today we're going to start learning the songs about Christmas and Chanukah that we'll be performing at the pageant. Then we'll study our lines.'

'Isn't it wonderful that Cordelia and Maeve are making sure that everybody has a speaking part?' Alvirah whispered.

'Everybody? Well, let's hope it's a *short* speaking part,' Willy replied.

Alvirah smiled. 'You don't mean that.'

'Want to bet?'

'Sshh.' She patted his hand as Sister Maeve Marie read off the names of the children who would be assigned to tell the story of Chanukah. 'Rachel, Barry, Sheila . . .'

Cordelia appeared from downstairs and, with her practiced eye, glanced over the children. Seeing mischief about, she walked over to Jerry, the lively seven-year-old who was poking the six-year-old seated next to him.

She tapped him lightly. 'Keep that up, and I'll find a new Saint Joseph,' she warned, then turned and joined Alvirah and Willy. 'When I got back, there was another message from Pablo Torres,' she said. 'He'd gone to bat for us, and I do believe he tried his best, but he says there was no way he could get an extension on keeping this place open. I think he was as happy as I was to hear about Bessie's townhouse. He knows the block and said he's sure there won't be any problem transferring our operation there. We can even take in more kids.'

One of the volunteer salespeople at the thrift shop came rushing up the stairs. 'Sister, Kate Durkin is on the phone, asking to talk to you. Hurry; she's crying her eyes out.'

CHAPTER SIX

No traces remained of the festive luncheon they had enjoyed only a few hours earlier. But once again, Willy, Alvirah, Monsignor Ferris and Sister Cordelia sat at the same table they had dined at earlier in the day. Kate was with them, quietly weeping.

'I spoke to the Bakers an hour ago,' she said. I told them that I was turning the house over to Home Base and that I couldn't renew their lease.'

'And you say they produced a new will?' Willy asked incredulously.

'Yes. They said Bessie had changed her mind, that she hadn't been a bit happy at the prospect of having the house wrecked by a bunch of kids. They also told me that she said the repairs Vic has made and the painting he's done showed her that they'd keep the house in pristine condition, just the way she wanted it. You know how much she loved this house.'

She married the judge to get it, Alvirah thought wryly. 'When did she sign it?'

'Just a few days ago, on November 30th.'

'She showed me the previous will when I stopped in to see her on November 27th,' Monsignor Ferris said. 'She seemed quite happy with it then. That was when she asked

45

me to make sure that Kate could stay in the apartment after she transferred the house to the Home Base program.'

'Bessie left me an income, and according to the new will, I'm allowed to live in the apartment in the *Bakers'* home rent free. As though I'd stay here with those people!' The tears now ran freely down Kate's face. 'I can't believe Bessie would do this to me. To leave this house to perfect strangers like that. She knew I didn't like the Bakers. And to get an apartment somewhere else is impossible. You know what the prices are in Manhattan.'

Kate's scared and she's angry and she's hurt, Alvirah thought. But even worse . . . She looked across the table and thought that for the first time since she'd known her, Cordelia looked her age.

Catching her sister-in-law's eye, she said, 'Cordelia, we'll think of something to keep Home Base going, I promise.'

Cordelia shook her head. 'Not in under four weeks,' she said. 'Not unless the age of miracles isn't over.'

Monsignor Ferris had been carefully studying the copy of the new will that Vic Baker had presented to Kate.

'From my experience, it looks absolutely legitimate,' he commented. 'It's on Bessie's stationery, we know that she was a good typist, and that certainly is her signature. Take a look,

Alvirah.'

Alvirah skimmed the page and a half and then reread it carefully. 'It certainly *sounds* like Bessie,' she admitted. 'Listen, Willy. "A home is like a child, and as one nears the end, it becomes important to surrender that home to the protection of those who would care for it in the most fitting manner. I cannot be comfortable knowing that the daily presence of many small children will totally change the appearance and character of the pristine house for which I have sacrificed so much." '

'Does she mean being married to Judge Maher?' Willy asked. 'He wasn't a bad little guy.'

Alvirah shrugged and continued to read. ' "Therefore I leave my home to Victor and Linda Baker, who will care for it in a manner suited to its genteel quality." '

'Genteel quality, indeed!' she snorted as she laid the will on the table. 'What could be more genteel than giving a helping hand to children?' She turned to the monsignor. 'Who witnessed this miserable piece of paper?'

'Two of the Bakers' friends,' Monsignor Ferris said. 'We'll get a lawyer, of course, just to see if there's anything to be done, but it certainly looks legitimate to me.'

Willy had been observing Alvirah for the past several minutes. 'Your brain cells are working, honey. I can tell,' he said.

47

'They sure are,' Alvirah conceded as she reached to turn on the microphone in her sunburst pin. 'This will may sound like Bessie in most ways, but Kate, did you ever hear her use the word "pristine"?'

'No, I don't think so,' Kate said slowly.

'What kind of things *did* she say when she talked about the house?' Alvirah asked, persisting in her probe of the new will.

'Oh, you know Bessie. She'd brag that you could eat a seven-course meal off the floor—that sort of thing.'

'Exactly,' Alvirah said. 'I know it looks bad, but every bone in my body says that this will is a phony. And Kate, Cordelia—I promise you that if there's any way to prove it, then I'll find that way. I'm on the job!'

CHAPTER SEVEN

Sister Maeve Marie had remained at Home Base and continued the rehearsal for the Christmas pageant, although in her mind she conjured up the worst possible scenario to explain why Sister Cordelia, Willy and Alvirah had raced off to see Kate Durkin.

'Something's gone wrong, and Kate's all upset,' was all that Cordelia had time to tell her before she left.

Was it possible that Kate had been robbed or mugged? Maeve Marie wondered. She knew that sometimes felons would look through the death notices in the paper and would burglarize the deceased's home when they thought the bereaved were at the funeral. A former New York City cop herself, with four policemen brothers, Maeve Marie thought instantly of potential criminal activity.

All the children at Home Base had been assigned their parts for the pageant and told to practice their lines at home. The Chanukah story would be recited at the beginning of the pageant, immediately followed by the Chanukah song.

Next would come the scene in which the decree from Caesar Augustus was read, proclaiming a census and telling everyone to

49

go to the village of his ancestors to be registered.

The play had been written by Cordelia and Alvirah, and Maeve Marie had complimented them on including so many speaking parts in that first scene. The kids loved that. Plus the lines were both simple and familiar.

'But my father's village is so far away.'

'It is such a long journey, and there is no one to care for the children.'

'We must find someone, because nothing is more important than that our children are safe.'

Cordelia had confessed that she was taking a few liberties with some of the dialogue, but she had invited the housing inspectors to the pageant and she wanted to be sure to get the message across to them: *Nothing is more important than that our children are safe.*

The only children who had not been assigned lines at random were the three wise men, the shepherds, the Virgin Mary and Saint Joseph. The ones selected for those parts were the best singers in the group and would lead the singing in the stable scene.

Jerry Nuñez, the biggest cutup among the younger children, was to be Saint Joseph, and Stellina Centino, a grave and oddly composed seven-year-old, was Mary.

Stellina and Jerry lived on the same block, and Jerry's mother picked up both children at the end of the day. 'Stellina's mama took off

50

for California when she was a baby,' Mrs. Nuñez explained to the nuns. 'And her dad is away a lot. Her great-aunt Lilly raised her, but now lately Lilly's been sick a lot, poor woman. And she worries so much. You wouldn't believe how she worries about Stellina. She says, "Gracie, I'm eighty-two; I gotta live another ten years anyhow so I can raise her. That's my prayer." '

Stellina is such a beautiful child, Maeve thought as she blocked out the final tableau for the pageant. Curly dark-blond hair that was clasped at the nape of her neck by a barrette fell down her back. Her porcelain complexion was enhanced by wide dark-brown eyes, fringed with long black lashes.

Jerry, never one to be still, began to make faces at one of the shepherds. Before Maeve Marie had a chance to admonish him, Stellina said, 'Jerry, when you are Saint Joseph, you have to be very good.'

'Okay,' Jerry agreed instantly, assuming a frozen posture of almost exaggerated decorum.

'The chorus of angels will begin to sing, the shepherds will see the angels and listen, and you, Tommy, will point to them and . . . then what do you say?' Sister Maeve Marie asked.

'I say, "Shark, the hellish angels sing," ' six-year-old Tommy suggested.

Sister Maeve Marie tried not to smile. Lead

us not into Penn Station, she thought—that's what my brothers used to tell me to say. Tommy had a smart-aleck big brother at home; chances were, he had been coaching his younger brother. 'Tommy, you have to get it right, and if you don't listen, you can't be the head shepherd,' she said firmly.

The rehearsal ended at six. Not a bad first practice, Maeve Marie decided as she complimented the children on their performances. The nice thing was that the kids were enjoying it.

She had enjoyed it as well, although the pleasure she took in seeing the children learn their parts was tempered by her concern and growing sense of unease: *Where was Cordelia, and what had gone wrong?*

As she helped to sort out jackets and mittens and scarves, Maeve noticed that, as usual, Stellina had carefully hung up her beautifully tailored blue winter jacket, which, the little girl had proudly explained, her nonna had made for her.

By six-thirty all the children except Jerry and Stellina were gone, most having waited for an adult or older sibling to walk them home. At quarter of seven, Sister Maeve Marie brought the two of them downstairs to the thrift shop, which was closed now. Five minutes later, Gracie Nuñez hurried in.

'My boss,' she said, rolling her eyes. 'We had

to get out some skirts. Two of the girls didn't show. Woulda been worth my job to tell her I had kids to worry about. God bless you, Sister. You have no idea what it means to know that the kids are safely with you. Jerry, say good night and thank you to Sister.'

Stellina did not need to be reminded. 'Good night, Sister,' she said quietly. 'And thank you very much.' Then with a rare smile she added, 'Nonna is so happy that I'm to be the Blessed Mother. She listens to me recite my lines every night, and when she does, she calls me Madonna.'

Maeve locked the door behind them and quickly began turning off the lights. Cordelia must either still be with Kate Durkin or she stopped in for a visit with some of the old girls, Maeve decided. She sighed with concern over what kind of news she would hear when she got home.

As she was putting on her coat she heard a tapping on the front window. She turned to see the face of a man who appeared to be fortyish, his features illuminated by the streetlight. Maeve stared at him with an ex-cop's intuitive sense of unease.

'Sister, is my little girl still here? I mean Stellina Centino,' he called.

Stellina's *father*! Maeve hurried to the door and opened it. With professional detachment she studied the thin-faced man, immediately

53

distrusting both his vague good looks and his hangdog expression. 'I'm sorry, Mr. Centino,' she said coolly, 'we didn't expect you. Stellina went home as usual with Mrs. Nuñez.'

'Oh, yeah, okay,' Lenny Centino said. 'I forgot. My job keeps me out of town a lot. Okay, Sister, I'll see you next week. I plan to be picking her up some nights. Take her to dinner and maybe even a movie. I wanna give Star a treat. I'm proud of her. She's turning into some good looking kid.'

'You should be proud. She's a beautiful child in every way,' Maeve Marie said shortly. She stood in the doorway and watched him leave. She sensed something disturbing and unsettling about that man.

Still troubled by concern for Sister Cordelia, she made a final check of the premises, turned on the security system and walked home through the dusting of snow that was promising to turn into another full-blown storm.

*   *   *

She found Sister Cordelia sitting with Sister Bernadette and Sister Catherine, two elderly retired nuns who shared their apartment-convent. 'Maeve, I confess to being weary to the soul,' Cordelia said, and then proceeded to tell her about the newfound will left by Bessie

54

Durkin Maher.

Instantly suspicious, Maeve asked questions about the new document: 'Aside from the use of the word "pristine," is there anything to suggest the will is a fake?'

Cordelia smiled wanly. 'Only Alvirah's instinct,' she said.

Sister Bernadette, who would be ninety on her next birthday, had been nodding in an easy chair. 'Alvirah's instinct, and something the Lord told us, Cordelia,' she said. 'You all know what I mean.'

Smiling at their puzzled expressions, she murmured, ' "Suffer the little children to come unto me." I don't think Bessie would have forgotten that, however house proud she was.'

CHAPTER EIGHT

Stellina kept the key to the apartment in a zippered pocket of her coat. Nonna had given it to her but had made her promise that she would never tell anyone it was there. Now she always used it when she got home so Nonna wouldn't have to get up if she was resting.

It used to be that when she came home from school she would find Nonna sewing in the small room where Daddy always slept when he was home. Then they'd have milk and cookies, and if Nonna had clothes to deliver, or someone to fit for a hem or a new dress, Stellina would accompany her great-aunt and help carry the bags and boxes to the ladies' homes.

But Nonna had been going to the clinic a lot lately, and that was why Mrs. Nuñez had suggested Stellina should be at Home Base each day after school.

Some nights, if Nonna was feeling well, Stellina would arrive home to find her in the kitchen, dinner cooking on the stove and the apartment filled with the good, warm smell of pasta sauce. But tonight she found Nonna lying in bed, with her eyes closed. Stellina could see though that she wasn't asleep, because her lips were moving. She's probably praying, Stellina thought. Nonna prayed a lot.

Stellina bent down to kiss her. 'Nonna, I'm home.'

Nonna opened her eyes and sighed. 'I was so worried. Your papa came home. He said he was going to Home Base. He said he wanted to take you out. I don't want you to go out with him. If ever he shows up there, asking for you, say that Nonna wants you to go home with Mrs. Nuñez.'

'Daddy's home?' Stellina asked, trying to hide her distress at the news. She wouldn't tell even Nonna that she was sorry he had reappeared, but she was. Whenever Daddy was home, he and Nonna argued a lot. And Stellina didn't like to go out with him, either, because sometimes they visited people and he would argue with them too. Sometimes the people gave him money and he'd argue about that, usually saying that something he gave them was worth a lot more than the money he'd received.

Nonna leaned on her elbow, sat up, then got out of bed very slowly. 'You must be hungry, *cara*. Come. I'll fix dinner for you.'

Stellina reached out her arm to help steady Nonna as she got up.

'Such a good girl,' Nonna murmured as she headed into the kitchen.

Stellina was hungry, and Nonna's pasta was always so good, but tonight it was hard for her to eat because of her concern for her great-aunt. Nonna looked so worried, and her breathing was fast, as though she had been running.

The click of the lock in the front door told them that Daddy was home. Immediately Nonna began to frown, and Stellina's mouth went dry. She knew that there would be an argument soon.

Lenny came into the kitchen and ran over to Stellina and picked her up. He swung her around and kissed her. 'Star, baby,' he said. 'I've missed you.'

Stellina tried to pull away. He was hurting her.

'Put her down, you roughneck!' Nonna shouted. 'Get out of here! Stay out of here! You're not welcome! Go away! Leave us alone!'

Lenny didn't display his usual anger. He just smiled. 'Aunt Lilly, maybe I *will* go for good, but if I do, I'll take Star with me. Neither you nor anyone else can stop me. Don't forget, I'm her daddy.'

Then he turned around and went out, slamming the door behind him. Stellina could see that Nonna was trembling, and there was perspiration on her forehead. 'Nonna, Nonna, it's all right,' she said. 'He won't take me away.

Nonna began to cry. 'Stellina,' she said, 'if I ever get sick and can't be here with you, you must never, go away with your daddy. I will ask Mrs. Nuñez to take care of you. But *promise* me, never go away with him. He is not a good man. He gets in trouble.'

As Stellina tried to comfort her, she heard her great-aunt whisper, 'He is the father. He is the guardian. Dear God, dear God, *what am I to do*?'

She wondered why her Nonna was crying.

CHAPTER NINE

As usual when she was trying to solve a possible crime, Alvirah did not sleep the sleep of the just. From the time she and Willy turned out the light following the eleven o'clock news, which they had watched in bed, Alvirah was restless. She spent the next six hours dozing, her light sleep filled with vague, unsettling dreams; then she woke with a start.

Finally at five-thirty, deciding to take pity on Willy, who had frequently mumbled in his sleep, 'Are you all right, honey?' she got up, put on her favorite old chenille robe, fastened on her sunburst pin with its tiny concealed recording microphone, got her pen and the tabbed notebook in which she kept the record of her ongoing investigations, made herself a cup of tea, settled down at the small dining table overlooking Central Park, turned on the microphone in her pin and began to think out loud.

'It's not beyond Bessie, who was always a true stickler and pain in the neck about her house, to leave it to people who she thought would keep it up a certain way. I mean, it's not as though she was throwing her sister out. After all, she did make sure that Kate would have the upstairs apartment, which is where she had planned to live anyway when she donated the ownership of the house to Home Base.'

Alvirah's jaw jutted out unconsciously as she went on. 'Bessie was never one to fall all over children, as I recall. In fact, I remember when someone asked her if she was sorry she hadn't had a family, she said, "People with children and people without them feel sorry for each other." '

For a moment Alvirah paused, thinking how much she and Willy would have loved to have had a family. By now her grandchildren would probably he the age of the kids she'd seen yesterday at Home Base. She shook her head. Well, never mind. It wasn't to be, she reminded herself briskly.

'So let's assume,' she went on, 'that Bessie really did get upset at the prospect of kids running around her precious house and getting finger marks on the walls and scratches on the woodwork, and, of course, by knowing that the furniture she'd been polishing since she went to work for the judge and his wife fifty years ago would he replaced by kids' paraphernalia.'

Remembering to check the microphone, Alvirah pushed the STOP, REWIND and PLAY buttons, and listened for a moment to the tape.

It's working, she told herself gratefully, and I sound as if I'm working up a head of steam.

Well, I am! she decided.

Clearing her throat, she resumed her indignant recital. 'So the only real clue we have so far to show that this new will might be false is that Bessie was never known to use the word "pristine."'

She picked up her pen and turned to the next unused section of her loose-leaf notebook, the one that followed 'The case of the death of Trinky Callahan.' At the top of the page, she wrote 'The case of Bessie's will,' then entered the first item in her investigation: 'Use of the word "pristine."'

Now Alvirah began to write quickly. Witnesses to the will: Who were they? What were their backgrounds? Time: The will was signed November 30th. Did Kate meet the witnesses? What did she think was going on if she was there and they asked to see Bessie?

Now I'm using the old gray matter, Alvirah thought. She had recently been rereading Agatha Christie's Hercule Poirot books. While working on the crimes she had helped to solve, she had tried to follow his method of deductive reasoning.

As she made the last entry in her plan of action, Alvirah looked at the clock: seven-thirty—time to close the notebook and turn off the microphone, she decided. Willy would be awake soon, and she wanted to have breakfast ready for him.

Then, sometime today, I have to sit down alone with Kate and go over these questions with her, she thought.

Suddenly another idea came to her, and she snapped the microphone on again. Since she had written that first article for the *New York Globe* about visiting Cypress Point Spa after winning the lottery, she and the editor there, Charley Evans, had become fast friends. He could get the lowdown on Vic and Linda Baker for her right away. 'The little gray cells are really waking up,' she announced. 'It's time to get the *Globe* researchers to dig up the dirt on the Bakers. Dollars to donuts, this isn't the first time that pair of phonies pulled a fast one.'

*   *   *

The 7:00 A.M. Mass at St. Clement's usually had an attendance of about thirty people, mostly the older, retired parishioners. But now that it was the season of Advent, the number attending was at least double that. In his brief homily, Monsignor Ferris spoke about Advent as the season of waiting. 'We are in the time when we anticipate the birth of the Savior,' he said. 'We anticipate the moment in Bethlehem when Mary gazed for the first time at her infant Son.'

A faint sob from the congregation riveted

his attention on the pew near the painting of Bishop Santori. The pretty young woman whom he had noticed earlier, standing across the street from the rectory, sat there. Her face was buried in her hands, and her shoulders were shaking. I have got to make her talk to me, he thought, but then he saw her reach into her purse, put on dark glasses and slip down the aisle and out the door.

*   *   *

At nine-thirty, Kate Durkin began going through everything left in her late sister's room. It would be a crying shame just to leave Bessie's clothes hanging in the closet when so many people need something to wear, she decided.

The four-poster bed which for eight years Bessie had shared with Judge Aloysius Maher, and from which she had gone to her Maker, seemed somehow to stand in silent reproach as Kate took dresses and jackets from the closet. Some of the items she recognized as being at least twenty years old. Bessie was always telling me that there was no point in giving them away, because maybe I could use them someday, Kate thought. What she didn't seem to realize is that I'd have had to grow five inches for any of them to fit. It's a wonder she didn't leave *them* to Linda Baker too, she thought bitterly.

The memory of yesterday's sudden revelations, and the surprise will, made Kate's eyes fill. As she impatiently brushed away a tear and glanced at Bessie's desk, the typewriter caught her eye. It seemed to her that there was something she should remember, but what was it?

She did not have time to think about what could have triggered her subconscious, however; having heard a sound behind her, she turned to find Vic and Linda standing in the doorway.

'Oh, Kate,' Linda said sweetly. 'I'm so glad you're clearing Bessie's things out of the room for us.'

The downstairs bell rang. 'I'll get it,' Vic Baker announced.

You're not taking over yet, Kate said to herself as she quickly followed him down the stairs.

A moment later, Kate saw the welcome sight of Alvirah on the front steps and heard her ask, 'Is Kate Durkin, the lady of the house, on these pristine premises?'

CHAPTER TEN

Lenny had gotten back to the apartment at midnight and tiptoed to his bedroom—mostly cleared of the clothing Lilly was mending—and gone to bed.

When he woke up at nine the next morning, he was surprised to hear the sound of voices in the other bedroom, then realized it was Saturday and Star had no school.

It also meant that Aunt Lilly probably was still in bed if she wasn't at Mass. She never had been the same after a bad fall last summer. She tried to tell him she was fine, but he had overheard her telling a neighbor that the doctor thought a blackout had been caused by a small stroke. Whatever had caused it, he definitely had seen a big difference in Lilly since he last had been here in September.

He had told her that he'd been in Florida, working for a delivery company. She responded that she was happy to know he had a regular job, and that he shouldn't worry about Stellina. Sure, I shouldn't worry about Star, he thought. Aunt Lilly would be happy if I never showed up here again.

Well, part of what I told her was true, he thought as he reached for a cigarette. I *did* make deliveries. Deliveries of little packages that made people happy. But it was getting too risky down there, so he thought he would come back to New York, pick up some small-time action and get to know Star. I'm just a nice, concerned single father, living in a respectable building with an old aunt, he thought. And that's good, because this way when Lilly closes her eyes for good, Star and I will at least know each other real well. Who knows? I might even be able to put her to work for me.

He thought over the situation as he puffed his cigarette down to the stub, ground it out in a tray with sewing supplies, then decided to light another one to settle his nerves before he faced Aunt Lilly.

Even when Star had still been an infant, and he would take her for an outing in her carriage, Lilly had been suspicious every time. Lenny smiled at the memory of all the goods he had been able to deliver, while people smiled and cooed at his beautiful baby. But when he got home, Lilly always peppered him with questions. 'Where did you walk? Where did you take her? Her blankets smell of smoke. I'll kill you if you took her to a bar.' She was always after him.

He knew, though, that he would have to be careful and not get Lilly all worried about the little girl. All he needed was to have his aunt get some crazy idea, like trying to trace Star's

68

mother, his supposed girlfriend who'd gone to California.

Through some of his connections he had managed to get a forged birth certificate for Star. The letter pinned to her blanket had said she was of Irish and Italian descent, which worked out fine. So I'm Italian and her mother was Irish, Lenny had decided, and told his source to fill out the mother's name as Rose O'Grady. He had thought of the song about Rosie O'Grady, which he liked when he was younger. He remembered some Irish kid in his class used to sing it.

Lilly would have a hell of a job trying to trace a Rose O'Grady in California, Lenny thought—it's a common name and a very big state—but any kind of inquiry was potential trouble, and he wasn't going to let it happen. He would have to start looking more like the concerned parent if he hoped to calm Lilly down.

After yawning, stretching, scratching his shoulder blade and pushing back his lank, dark hair, Lenny got out of bed. He pulled on some jeans, stuffed his feet into sneakers, remembered to put on a T-shirt, then went down the hall to his aunt's bedroom.

The door was open, and he could see that, as he had expected, Lilly was propped up in bed. The room was neat but crowded, with Star's narrow cot wedged between the bed and the wall.

As he stood in the doorway, Star's back was to him, and Lilly was listening to her recite the lines from her part in the Christmas pageant. Lilly had not noticed him, so he stood back quietly while Star, sitting cross-legged on the bed, her back ramrod-straight, her curly, dark-blond hair escaping from the barrette, said, 'Oh, Joseph, it does not matter that they would not accept us at the inn. The stable will give us shelter, and the child will wait no longer to come to us.'

'*Bella, bella*, Madonna,' Lilly said, 'The Blessed Mother will be very pleased that you are to portray her.' She sighed and grasped Stellina's hands. 'And today I will begin to sew a white tunic and a blue veil for you, to wear in the pageant, Stellina *cara* . . .'

Lilly looks like she should be in the hospital, Lenny thought with a twinge of alarm. Her skin was gray, and he could see beads of perspiration on her forehead. He was about to ask her how she was feeling, but stopped and frowned as he glanced at the top of the dresser. It was covered with a display of religious relics and statues of the Holy Family and Saint Francis of Assisi. Those he was used to—she always had been super-religious—but he still regretted that years ago Lilly had found the silver cup from which he had pried the diamond.

70

There'd been such a stink in the papers about it at the time, because the cup that had been stolen had been the chalice of a famous bishop. He knew it wouldn't have been smart to try to hock it at the time; it was too big a risk for the few bucks it might bring. Instead, he had tossed it in the back of his closet, figuring he'd get rid of it at some point, like when he was in another city.

Then Lilly had gone on one of her cleaning rampages and found it, said it looked like a chalice, so he had to quickly come up with some dumb story about how it had belonged to Star's mother, Rose. He told Lilly that her uncle, a priest, left it to her when he died. So, of course, Lilly polished it so that the silver gleamed like new and put it up with her statues.

Oh well, it made her happy, Lenny thought, and not being able to hock it at the time probably kept him from getting in trouble. It was a cinch nobody was looking for it now, though, and he wondered how much it would bring. At least Lilly hadn't found the note that had been pinned to Star's blanket. He had held on to that just in case anybody ever questioned where she came from, and he had to prove he hadn't kidnapped her.

He had wedged the note into a crack between the top shelf and wall of his closet. Lilly could never reach it, even when she used a dust mop to get at the shelf.

With a shrug, Lenny turned and went into the kitchen to check the refrigerator and grocery cabinet for breakfast makings. Lean pickings, he thought. Lilly obviously hadn't been shopping lately. He jotted a list of things to buy, grabbed his jacket and went back to her room.

This time he entered the room with a big 'Good morning, how are my girls?' Solicitously he asked Lilly how she felt, told Star to be sure to do her homework and announced that he was on his way to the store.

After he rattled off the list of items he intended to buy, Lilly looked at him suspiciously but then relented and added a couple of things.

Outside, the air was sharp, and he regretted not wearing his cap. He would go to the diner and get a decent breakfast first, he decided. While he was there he would make a phone call to let his local sources know he was available to do their errands again, which he was confident they'd be glad to hear.

And once dear Aunt Lilly is out of the picture, I'll be able to make little Star a part of my operation, Lenny thought. She'll be a great partner for me—who'd ever guess?

Yes, working hand in hand, Star and her daddy will have a good delivery business going, he promised himself.

CHAPTER ELEVEN

Sondra felt the eyes of the monsignor following her when she fled from church. Trying to muffle her sobs, she jogged back to the hotel. Once there, she showered, ordered coffee, then pressed cold wet cloths against her swollen eyes. I've *got* to stop crying, she told herself fiercely. I've got to stop crying! The concert was so very important, and she had to be prepared.

At nine o'clock she was scheduled to go to her rented studio in Carnegie Hall and practice for five hours. She had to get herself together. She knew she had been off form yesterday, distracted, not playing nearly to her usual standard.

But how can I think about anything but the baby? Sondra kept asking herself What happened to my little girl? For these past seven years she had been picturing her living with a wonderful couple who maybe hadn't had a child of their own and who loved and worshiped her. But now she had no idea who had found her—or even if she had been found at all.

She looked in the mirror. What a mess! she thought. Her face was blotchy and her eyes swollen. There was nothing more she could do about her eyes, she decided, but her long, delicate fingers moved deftly as she dabbed base makeup over her face to cover the evidence of her tears.

I'll walk past the rectory again this afternoon, she decided. That thought at least was calming. It was the last place where she had seen her baby, and she felt near to her when she was there. Also, when she prayed at the portrait of Bishop Santori, something of the same peace her grandfather had described feeling when he prayed there all those years ago seemed to come to her. Her prayer was not to have the baby back. I don't have the right to ask for that, she thought. just give me a way to know she's safe, and *loved*. That's all I ask.

She had taken a parish bulletin from St. Clement's, and now she dug it out of the pocket of her jogging jacket. Yes, she saw there was a five o'clock Mass. She would attend it, but she would arrive a little late. That way the monsignor wouldn't have a chance to try to speak to her. Then she would slip out again before it was over.

As she twisted her dark-blond hair, gathering it up at the back of her head, she wondered if the baby had grown to look even a little bit like her.

74

CHAPTER TWELVE

Over a pot of tea and a generous slice of Kate Durkin's melt-in-your-mouth crumb cake, Alvirah began to form a plan of action aimed at saving the townhouse from the clutches of the Bakers.

'Isn't it awful to think that you have to keep your voice down in your own home?' Kate asked. 'Those two are always pussyfooting around. Just before you arrived, my heart almost stopped when I turned around and saw the two of them watching me. That's why I closed the door just now.' Then she glanced at the copy of her sister's will and sighed. 'I guess I can't do anything about it, though. They seem to have everything in their favor.'

'We'll see about that,' Alvirah said firmly as she turned on the microphone in her sunburst pin. 'I've got a whole bunch of questions for you, so let's get started. Now, Monsignor came over to see you on Friday the 27th. He said that there was no question in his mind that Bessie would be leaving the house to you, although he did know that she was unhappy at the prospect of having kids mess it up.'

Kate nodded. Her soft blue eyes—magnified by large, round glasses—were thoughtful. 'You know Bessie,' she said. 'She was so set in her ways, and she complained about how nothing would be the same here with a bunch of kids running around. But I remember that then she sort of laughed and said, 'Well, at least by then I won't be here to clean up after them—that'll be *your* job, Kate.'

'That was Friday the 27th, right?' Alvirah asked. 'How was Bessie over the weekend?'

'Tired. Her heart was just giving out, and she knew it. She had me get out her blue print dress and have it pressed. Then she told me that when her time came I should put her pearls on her. She said they really weren't valuable, but they were the only jewelry the judge ever gave her, other than the wedding band, of course, and that neither one was worth leaving to anyone. Then she said, 'You know, Kate, Aloysius was really a good man. If I'd married him when I was young, I probably would have had a family of my own and wouldn't have had a chance to get so fussy about scratches and finger marks.'

'That was Saturday?' Alvirah asked.

'Actually, Sunday.'

'Then on Monday she supposedly had the new will witnessed. Didn't you hear her banging away on the typewriter before that? What did you think when the witnesses came in for the signing?'

'I never saw them,' Kate replied, shaking her head. 'You know how I always volunteer for a

76

couple of hours at the hospital on Monday and Friday afternoons. Bessie would never hear of me not going. She seemed pretty good when I left—she was sitting downstairs in her chair in the parlor, watching television. I remember she said she'd be glad to be rid of me for a few hours. That she was feeling all right and getting sick of me looking worried.'

'And where was she when you got home?'

'Why, still there, watching one of her soap operas.'

'All right. Now, the next thing I want to do is talk to those two witnesses.' Alvirah studied the last page of the will. 'Do you have any idea who they are?'

'I've never heard of them,' Kate replied.

'Well, I intend to call on them. Their address is here under their signatures. James and Eileen Gordon, on West Seventy-ninth.' Alvirah looked up as Vic Baker pushed open the door to the dining room without knocking.

'Having a nice little cup of tea?' he asked with forced joviality.

'We *were*,' Alvirah said.

I just wanted to let you know that we're going out for a bit, but when we come back we'll be glad to help you carry dear Bessie's clothing downstairs.'

'We're going to take good care of Bessie's possessions,' Alvirah told him. 'You don't have to worry about a thing.'

77

The cheery expression disappeared from Baker's face. 'I happened to have overheard what you just said about speaking to the witnesses, Mrs. Meehan,' he snapped. 'I'll be happy to give you their phone number. You'll find them to be perfectly responsible people.' He fished in his pocket. 'As a matter of fact, I have their card.'

Baker handed Alvirah the card, then turned and walked out, pulling the door closed behind him with a bang. Both women turned and watched as the door slowly swung open again.

'It won't stay closed,' Kate said. 'He's one of those fixit guys who talks a good game, and obviously he impressed Bessie. The truth is he can use a paintbrush, but that's about it.' She pointed to the door. 'Did you notice he didn't turn the knob just now? He pushed the door open. It used to stick, so he shaved it down. Now it doesn't even catch. Same thing in the parlor—that's become a swinging door.' She sniffed.

Alvirah was only half listening. She was studying the card Vic Baker had given her. 'This is a business card,' she said. 'The Gordons have a real estate agency. Now how about *that*?'

*   *   *

'He may not be able to fix doors, but he sure
78

can get a will done,' Alvirah told Willy late that afternoon, when he arrived home and found her sitting dejectedly in the living room of their apartment. 'Jim and Eileen Gordon seem like straight arrows to me.'

'How did they happen to become witnesses to the will?'

'According to them, almost accidentally. It seems that Vic Baker has been looking at townhouses and condos ever since he moved here nearly a year ago. They say they've taken him out a number of times, to look at homes. He had an appointment with them at three o'clock on the 30th, to see some place on Eighty-first Street, and while they were there, Linda apparently called him on his cell phone. She told him Bessie wasn't feeling well and wanted to get her new will witnessed. Vic asked the Gordons if they would mind. So the Gordons went along, and—now this is the part that's so upsetting—they tell me Vic and Linda both nearly fell over in a faint when Bessie read the will to them before she signed it.'

'If the Gordons have been taking Baker out looking at real estate they must have checked his credit,' Willy said. 'Did you ask about that?'

'They did. Believe it or not, the Bakers are well fixed.' She attempted a smile. 'Cordelia keep you busy today?'

'I never got up for air. A pipe broke at the thrift shop, and I couldn't fix it until I turned

79

off all the water. Good thing it was Saturday and there were no kids upstairs.'

'Well, that won't be a problem soon,' Alvirah said with a sigh. 'And unless my gray cells come up with something I'm missing, there won't be a place for them anywhere.' She reached up and flipped on the microphone in her sunburst pin. Deftly she rewound the last bit of tape, then pressed the PLAY button.

Eileen Gordon's pleasant voice was clear and easy to understand. 'The last thing Mrs. Maher said was that now she could die in peace, knowing her home would remain pristine.'

'I swear that miserable word "pristine" is the key,' Alvirah said as the dejected look left her face. 'What is that expression Monsignor always uses when he's suspicious about something?'

'"Something is rotten in the state of Denmark,"' Willy replied. 'Is that what you mean?'

'That's it. In this case, though, I think there's something rotten on the Upper West Side,' Alvirah said. 'And I'm going to keep dropping in on the Gordons and talking to them until I find out just what it is. I think they're good people, but still there's something fishy about them just happening to be witnesses. Maybe they're very good actors, and I'm falling for their baloney.'

'Talking about baloney,' Willy said, 'let's have an early dinner. I'm starving.'

*   *   *

They were going out the door at six-thirty when Monsignor Ferris phoned. 'Kate was at Mass,' he said. 'She told me you went to see the witnesses. How did it go?'

Alvirah gave him a fast rundown, assuring him she wasn't giving up. Then, before saying good-bye, she added, 'Has that young woman we saw yesterday been around again?'

'She was here twice today. This morning she came to Mass, then left during the sermon. She seemed to be in great distress over something. Then I spotted her at the five o'clock, but again I didn't have a chance to talk to her. Alvirah, you said you thought she looked familiar. Any idea who she is or where you might have seen her before? I'd really like to try to help her.'

'I've been searching my mind, but so far I haven't come up with it,' Alvirah replied regretfully. 'But give me time. The thing is, I am sure I've seen her picture somewhere, but I just can't place it.'

Two hours later, as she and Willy passed Carnegie Hall on their way home from dinner, she stopped in the middle of a sentence and pointed. 'Willy, look. It's that girl.'

A glass-covered poster for the Christmas concert included photographs of the artists who would be performing, including Plácido Domingo, Kathleen Battle, Yo-Yo Ma, Emanuel Ax and Sondra Lewis.

Alvirah and Willy went over to read the caption under Sondra Lewis's picture. Even in this photo she appeared sad-eyed and unsmiling. 'Why would a girl about to make her Carnegie Hall debut be so unhappy?' Willy asked, clearly puzzled.

'Obviously it has something to do with St. Clement's,' Alvirah told him. 'And I intend to figure out what that one's all about too.'

CHAPTER THIRTEEN

When she had been very little, Stellina had asked Nonna why she didn't have a mother like the other children. Nonna had said that Stellina's mother left her with her Daddy because when she was born her mother became very sick and had to go to California to try to get better. Nonna said that her mother had been very sad to leave her, that she had promised if she ever got better she would come to see her. But Nonna also told Stellina that she thought that might never happen, and that she personally believed that God had called Stellina's mother to heaven.

Then, just when Stellina was starting kindergarten, Nonna had showed her the silver chalice she had found in Daddy's closet and explained that her mother's uncle, a priest, had given it to Stellina's mother, and that she had left it for Stellina. Nonna explained that the cup had been used to celebrate Mass and was blessed in a very special way.

The cup became a talisman for Stellina, and sometimes when she was just going off to sleep and was thinking about her mother, wishing so much that she could see her, she would ask Nonna if she could hold it.

Nonna teased her about it at the time.

'Babies give up their security blankets, Stellina. Now that you're a big girl and going to school, you decide you need one,' she had said. But she always smiled and never refused to let Stellina hold the cup. Sometimes in English, sometimes in Italian, and frequently in a mixture of both, she would reassure this wonderful little girl, the only real gift her otherwise worthless nephew had given her. 'Ah, *bambina*,' Nonna would whisper, 'I will always take care of you.'

Stellina didn't tell Nonna that when she twined her fingers around the cup, it was as if she could feel her mother's hands still holding it.

On Sunday afternoon, as she watched Nonna sew the blue veil she was to wear in the pageant, Stellina had an idea. She would ask Nonna if she could take the cup to the pageant and pretend that as the Blessed Mother she was giving it to the Baby Jesus.

Nonna protested. 'Oh, no, Stellina. It might get lost, and besides, the Blessed Mother had no silver to give to the Baby Jesus. It wouldn't be right.'

Stellina didn't argue, but she knew she had to find a way to persuade Nonna to let her bring the cup to the stable. She knew exactly the prayer she would say when she brought it there: 'If my mother is still sick, please make her well, and please, please ask her to visit me just one time.'

*   *   *

At Manhattan's 24th Police Precinct, Detective Joe Tracy expressed keen interest in the fact that Lenny Centino had once again resurfaced. He remembered Lenny from an investigation he'd been involved with a few years back. He hadn't been able to tie him directly to the crime, which had involved the sale of drugs to minors, but he was certain that Lenny was one of the guilty parties.

Tracy's partner pointed out that the rap sheet on Lenny was minor league—just a few breaking and enterings, penny-ante stuff—but Tracy was convinced that it was only because Lenny had not been caught.

'Sure, he served a little time,' Tracy argued, 'juvenile detention twenty-five years ago, record expunged, but in my opinion he only learned new tricks of his trade. He was arrested a few times, but never indicted. We never could pin anything definite on him, but I always was sure he was distributing drugs to high school kids. I remember how I used to see him pushing his kid in her carriage all over the West Side. I heard later that the kid was just a cover-up—that he stashed his stuff in the carriage, right there with the baby.'

Tracy tossed his slim folder on Lenny

85

Centino back on the desk. 'Well, now that he's back, I'm going to keep my eye on him. If I see him with that little girl, I may just bring him in. He'll make a mistake eventually, and when he does, I intend to be there.'

CHAPTER FOURTEEN

On Monday morning, as she and Willy were eating breakfast, Alvirah answered the phone and was delighted to hear the welcome voice of her editor, Charley Evans, announce that, while they never had been convicted, Vic and Linda Baker were clearly world-class con artists.

'Wait a minute,' she interrupted. 'I want to record everything so I won't forget a word.' She ran to the bedroom, for her sunburst pin, turned on the microphone and hurried back. 'Okay, Charley, shoot,' she said as she held the pin to the phone.

'The Bakers make a habit of preying on elderly people with property,' Charley said. 'The most recent case was in Charlestown last year, where they got friendly with an old man worth a couple of million bucks. He apparently was mad at his daughter at the time, angry about the guy she married, but he never indicated that he intended to disinherit her. According to witnesses, these two crooks kept filling his ears with stories about his daughter and how she couldn't wait to get her hands on his money. Guess what?'

'They came up with a new will,' Alvirah suggested.

'You guessed it. The old guy left his daughter a few bucks and her mother's jewelry. Everything else went to the Bakers. You see, they were smart enough not to grab everything. That would have been easier to contest.'

'What about witnesses to the will?' Alvirah asked.

'Solid citizens, all of them.'

'That's about what I expected,' she said with a sigh.

'I found two or three other similar cases in the last ten years, but you get the idea. The wills have all been contested, but each time the Bakers won hands down.'

'They won't *this* time,' Alvirah vowed.

'I hope not, for your friend's sake, but here's a little free advice: Tell her to go down to Surrogates Court at 31 Chambers Street and file a notice of intent to contest because of undue influence. Otherwise the will could be probated in anywhere from a couple of days to a couple of months, depending on the judge. If she files the notice, it will at least delay transfer of assets. Who's the executor?'

'Vic Baker.'

'They thought of everything,' Charley commented. 'Okay, Alvirah, let me know if I can help, and don't forget—I want a column out of this.'

'You bet you'll get one, and I've got the

headline for it,' Alvirah said. 'Write it down: *EXPOSING THE SKUNKS*.'

Charley chuckled. 'Go for it, Alvirah. My money's on you.

*   *   *

Over her third cup of tea, Alvirah told Willy about the conversation. 'Now, honey,' Willy admonished, 'your jaw is sticking out six feet. I know you're going to do your best, but you've got to promise me you won't get into any danger. I'm getting too old to worry about your being pushed off terraces or drowned in bathtubs.'

'The Bakers aren't the type to do anything like that,' Alvirah said dismissively. 'They're not violent, just sneaky. What has Cordelia got lined up for you today?'

'Home Base,' Willy said, shaking his head. 'You know, honey, I have to agree with the inspectors. That place *is* falling apart. You can do just so much in the way of repairs with bubblegum and Elmer's glue. After that you need to call in the heavy machinery. But anyhow, I'm going to get in an hour's practice on the piano too. Cordelia heard me banging out "All Through the Night" when I was over there to fix that leak yesterday, and now she's decided to make that the closing song of the pageant and wants me to play it. She has some crazy idea that having me take part will show the kids that you can learn something new at any age.'

'That's wonderful!' Alvirah said, her face beaming.

'Well, I think it's a lousy idea,' Willy said, 'but kids aren't judgmental, and the parents will only be looking at their own kids, so maybe nobody'll even notice me . . . Anyhow, what are *you* up to?'

'I'm going to stop in on Kate. You know how it is. When someone dies, everyone comes around for a couple of days, then after the funeral, the person who's been left behind wakes up and it sinks in that she'll never see that face or hear that voice again. That's when friends are really needed, and doubly so in Kate's case, because she has to put up with those crooks as well as missing Bessie. Then after I see her, I'm going to see Monsignor Tom and tell him I know who the young woman is who's been hanging around St. Clement's.'

With her usual efficiency, Alvirah tidied the kitchen, made the bed, showered and then dressed, choosing one of the simple but elegant pantsuits her friend Baroness Min von Schreiber had helped her to buy on Min's last trip East. As Min constantly pointed out, left on her own, Alvirah gravitated to wildly inappropriate styles and colors, an opinion

90

Alvirah humbly accepted.

As she was about to go out, she paused long enough to listen to Willy at the piano, practicing 'All Through the Night.' Proudly she noted that he was playing with increasing skill. Her lips silently formed the words as he sang the verses. The line 'I my loving vigil keeping,' seemed to her almost like a prayer. Well, I'm keeping a vigil for you, Kate, she thought.

When she arrived at the townhouse, she was shocked to find a calm but resolute Kate, who announced that after much thought, she had decided to find some other place to live, even if it was only a furnished room. She said if Bessie wanted the Bakers to have her house, then so be it. Bessie's intentions had been clear, and she had left Kate the use of the apartment and an income. 'But I can't live in the same house as these people, Alvirah,' Kate said. 'Every time I think of Bessie, sick as she was, sitting at her desk and typing that will, then making sure to get witnesses in when she knew I'd be out—well, I just get a pain like a knife through me.'

'Kate, you just reminded me of something I hadn't thought of. The will was signed last Monday, November 30th, right? But it was dated November 28th.'

'Exactly. That was the day after Bessie told Monsignor she didn't like the idea of turning the house into a children's center. So even when she was joking with me about it over the weekend, saying it was going to be my problem dealing with all those children, she was sitting at that typewriter while I was out.'

'How often were you out last weekend?' Alvirah asked.

'Just to morning Mass both Saturday and Sunday. But Bessie was a fast typist. You know how proud she was of that. She could have typed that will in twenty minutes.'

'Oh, Kate!' Alvirah said. Her heart ached as she looked at her old friend. All the fight seemed to have left Kate. Her shoulders were slumped in defeat, and the spark that gave wiry strength to her small frame seemed to have been extinguished. Alvirah knew it was no use arguing with her —she had made up her mind. The best she could do was stall for time.

'Kate,' she said, 'just do me one favor. I've been making some calls about the Bakers. Already I've found out that they are known to be con artists. They've just never been arrested—yet! Give me till Christmas to prove that Bessie didn't write that will, and even though it looks like she signed it, I bet if she did, she never knew what she was signing.'

Kate's eyes widened. 'Oh, Alvirah, there's no way to prove that.'

'Yes, there is,' Alvirah said with a hearty

confidence she did not feel. 'And I already know where to start. As soon as I see Monsignor Tom, I'm going to the James and Eileen Gordon Real Estate Agency and tell them I'm hunting for a co-op. Those two are going to see a lot of me in the next couple of weeks. Maybe they're part of the Bakers' scheme, or maybe they've just had the wool pulled over their eyes, but one way or another, I'm going to find out which it is.'

CHAPTER FIFTEEN

Lenny Centino had managed to stay out of prison by not being too greedy. The deliveries he made of drugs were small-time and infrequent, so except for having attracted the unwanted attention of Detective Joe Tracy, he was never high on the hit list of any police officer. Also he never actually *sold* drugs, he just delivered them, which, if he were caught, carried a lighter sentence. The drugs had been paid for in advance, so he never handled the money either. He had earned a reputation among both dealers and users of being dependable, and of never dipping into the goods, so he was in demand.

Still, because he liked to limit his involvement with the always dangerous drug trade, Lenny worked off and on for a reputable liquor store. Making deliveries for them, he was able to scope out people's apartments. He was a gifted burglar—he always made his hit when he was sure people were out, and he never bothered with anything but jewelry and money.

His earlier, very satisfactory career of robbing poor boxes and votive candle offering boxes had ended with his theft at St. Clement's. The church's silent alarm and his unwitting kidnapping of Star had made him realize that he was getting too close to the edge. Now even the smaller churches were getting smart enough to put in silent alarms.

That was why it was with confidence in his own ability to survive that he let his contacts know that he was back in the city and once again available. Over a couple of beers on Monday afternoon he had bragged about what he'd been doing since September, helping to run a scam for a fake computer company. What Lenny did not know was that an undercover cop had infiltrated the group he was boasting to, and when the cop had filed his report at the precinct, Detective Tracy had picked up on it and now had Lenny under surveillance, which included a wiretap. What the police did not know was that Lenny feared just such a situation and had an exit planned. He had a stash of money from the last job, along with a fake identity and a hideout all arranged in Mexico. But since his return to New York, Lenny had added another element to the exit scenario. It was obvious that Aunt Lilly was dying. He was genuinely fond of Star, and she always had been an asset to his operation. She was also his good-luck charm, so he had decided that if he ever had to get out of the country, he'd take her with him.

And as he often told himself, 'I *am* her daddy, and it wouldn't be right to abandon her.'

Unspoken, but perhaps even more pertinent, was Lenny's awareness that a man traveling with a little girl would be unlikely to appear to anyone to be a crook on the run.

CHAPTER SIXTEEN

Sondra had promised herself that she wouldn't go near St. Clement's again. If Granddad weren't coming in for the concert, I'd go to the police right now, she thought. I can't live like this any longer. If someone found the baby in those few minutes, and read the note and decided to keep her, and she's being raised in New York, then there *might* be a fake birth certificate. It would have been easy enough for someone to claim the baby was delivered at home. In that hotel, no one knew that I had given birth—I never had a single pain.

All the pain has come afterwards, she reflected as she lay awake Sunday night. As dawn was breaking, she finally drifted off. After having slept for only a few hours, she awoke with a blinding headache.

She got up and listlessly put on her jogging clothes. A run might clear my head, she decided. I've got to be able to concentrate on practice today. I've done so many things wrong—I don't want to add ruining the concert for Granddad to the list.

She had promised herself that she would stay in Central Park today, but when she came near the northern end of the park, her feet turned west. Minutes later she was standing across the street from St. Clement's, remembering once again the moment when she had held her baby for the last time.

It had warmed up a little, and the street was busier, so she knew she couldn't dawdle for fear of drawing attention to herself. The snow that had been arctic white on Thursday was now almost fully melted, and the remaining dregs covered with soot.

It was very cold that night, she remembered, *and the snow on the sides of the street was icy. That secondhand stroller had a stain on the side. I scrubbed the inside, but it was so terribly shabby that I hated to lay the baby in it even for a minute. Someone at the hotel had thrown out the shopping bag I used as extra protection. I remember it had a Sloan's logo on it. I bought the bottles and formula at a Duane Reade pharmacy.*

Sondra felt a tap on her shoulder. Startled, she turned to see the concerned face of a somewhat plump, redheaded woman of about sixty. 'You need help, Sondra,' Alvirah said gently. 'And I'm the one to give it to you.'

        *   *   *

They took a cab back to Central Park South. Once in the apartment, Alvirah made a pot of tea and popped bread in the toaster.

'I'll bet you haven't had a bite to eat today,'

she said.

Once again close to tears, Sondra nodded in agreement. She felt a kind of unreality, coupled with a great sense of relief. Now that she was in this strange apartment with this strange woman, she felt comfortable.

She knew she was going to tell Alvirah Meehan about the baby, and she sensed just from Alvirah's presence that Alvirah would somehow find a way to help her.

*   *   *

Twenty minutes later, Alvirah told her firmly, 'Now listen, Sondra, the first thing you've got to do is to stop beating up on yourself. That was seven years ago; you were a kid. You didn't have a mother. You felt responsible to your grandfather. You had your baby all by yourself, but you planned for it and you planned well. You had clothes and formula and bottles all ready, and you saved every nickel so the baby would be born in New York because you knew you wanted to live here someday. You dressed the baby and put her, nice and warm and safe, in a stroller on the stoop of the church rectory. You had chosen the church that had saved your grandfather when he knew his arthritis was robbing him of the gift he had as a violinist. You phoned the rectory less than five minutes later, and you

101

thought the baby had been found by someone there.'

'Yes,' Sondra said, 'but suppose some kids just pushed the stroller away as a joke. Suppose the baby froze to death, and when someone found her, they didn't want to he blamed . . . Suppose—'

'Suppose some good people found her and she's now the light of their lives,' Alvirah said with a conviction she didn't feel. Good people would have called the police and *then* tried to adopt her, she thought. They wouldn't have kept quiet about it all these years.

'I can't ask more than that,' Sondra said. 'I don't deserve more than that, because I just don't know . . .'

'You deserve a lot more than you think you do. Give yourself credit,' Alvirah told her briskly. 'Now you've got to get on with your violin practice and give New York music lovers a treat. You leave the detecting to me.' Then, spontaneously, she added, 'Sondra, do you know how beautiful you are when you smile? You've got to do more of that, hear me?'

Over yet another cup of tea, bit by bit, she drew Sondra out.

'Can you imagine what it was like for my poor grandfather, living alone, a music critic and violin teacher, to be suddenly stuck with a ten-year-old child to raise?' Sondra asked, a smile playing around her lips. 'He had a very nice four-room apartment in a good building on Lake Michigan in Chicago, but still it was tiny, and he couldn't afford more space.'

'What did he do when you moved in?' Alvirah asked.

'He changed his whole life for me. He turned his study into a bedroom and gave me the big bedroom. Whenever he went out, he hired someone to come in and mind me and cook for me. I might add, Granddad loved to go out to dinner with his friends, and, of course, he went to many concerts. There were a lot of things he had loved to do that he gave up for me.'

'You're putting yourself down again,' Alvirah said, interrupting. I bet he was lonely before you came. I bet he took great comfort in having you with him.'

Sondra's smile got wider. 'Maybe, but the trade-off in having me as company was his freedom to come and go, all the little luxuries he had enjoyed.' The smile vanished. 'I guess I did make it up to him in a way. I *am* a good musician, a good violinist.'

'Bingo!' Alvirah said. 'You're finally saying something good about yourself.'

Sondra laughed. 'You know, Alvirah, you do have a way with words.'

'That's what my editor says,' Alvirah agreed. 'Okay, I get the picture. You felt the responsibility to succeed, you won the

103

scholarship, you met someone attractive and gifted, you'd just turned eighteen and you fell for him. He probably told you how crazy he was about you, and, let's face it, you were vulnerable. You didn't have a mother and father, or brothers and sisters. Instead you had a grandfather who by then was starting to get sick. Have I got it straight?

'Yes.'

'We know the rest. Let's skip to the present. No one as pretty and talented as you are lives in a vacuum. Have you got a boyfriend?'

'No.'

'Too quick an answer, Sondra, which means you *do* have one. Who is he?'

There was a long silence. 'Gary Willis. He's on the board of the Chicago Symphony,' Sondra said reluctantly. 'He's thirty-four, eight years older than I am, very successful, very handsome, very nice, and he wants to marry me.'

'So far, so good,' Alvirah volunteered. 'And you don't care about him?'

'I could. I'm just not ready for marriage. Right now I'm an emotional basket case—I know that. I'm afraid that if I *do* get married, I'll never be able to look at my newborn's face without knowing that I left its sibling in a shopping bag out in the cold. Gary has been very patient and understanding with me. You'll get to meet him. He's bringing my grandfather in for the concert.'

'I like the sound of him already,' Alvirah said. 'And don't forget, ninety percent of women today juggle husbands or families and careers. I know I did.'

Sondra looked around the tastefully furnished apartment and out over the spectacular view of Central Park. 'What do you do, Alvirah?'

'Right now, my career is lottery winner, problem solver and contributing columnist to the *New York Globe*. Until three years ago I was a spectacular cleaning woman.'

Sondra's chuckle indicated she wasn't sure whether to believe her or to take what she said as a joke, but Alvirah did not elaborate. Plenty of time later for the history of my life, she thought.

They got up together. 'I must get to practice,' Sondra said. 'I've got a coach coming today who has a reputation that sends chills down the spines of performers like me.'

'Well, you go and give it your all,' Alvirah said. 'I'm going to figure out a way to try to track down that baby of yours without anyone knowing who's doing it. I'll call you every day, I promise.'

'Alvirah, Granddad and Gary will be coming in the week before the concert. I know Granddad will want to go to St. Clement's. He'll be so sad to hear that Bishop Santori's chalice is missing. But in case we should run into Monsignor Ferris when we're there, will you talk to him first and explain that you and I have talked, and ask him please not to let Granddad know I've been hanging around the church?'

'Absolutely,' Alvirah said promptly.

When they walked through the living room, Sondra stopped at the piano, where *John Thompson's Book for Mature Beginners* was on the rack, open to 'All Through the Night.'

She stopped and played the melody with one hand. I'd forgotten all about that song; it's lovely, isn't it?' Without waiting for an answer, she played it again and softly sang, 'Sleep, my child, and peace attend thee, All through the night; Guardian angels God will send thee, All through the night.'

She stopped. 'Sort of appropriate, isn't it, Alvirah?' Her voice broke. 'I hope my baby found a guardian angel that night.' She looked suddenly as if she might cry.

'I'll call you,' Alvirah promised as Sondra rushed out.

CHAPTER SEVENTEEN

'Are you all through with me, Cordelia?' Willy asked wearily. 'Both toilets are working, but I would suggest you tell the kids not to throw wads of tissue in them. Think of those pipes as belonging in an old-age home. Which is where I feel I should be right now,' he added with a sigh.

'Nonsense,' Sister Cordelia said briskly. 'You're still a young man, William. Just wait till you get to be *my* age.' There was a ten-year difference between the siblings.

'Cordelia, the day you're a hundred, you'll still have more energy than a Rockette,' Willy told her.

'Speaking of which, I'm supposed to watch a run-through of the pageant. Come on, let's get upstairs. The kids will be going home soon,' Sister Cordelia said, grasping Willy by the arm and propelling him toward the staircase.

It was quarter of six, and the rehearsal for the pageant was in full swing. They had reached the final scene, in the stable. A solemn-faced Stellina was kneeling across from a merry-eyed Jerry Nuñez, over the folded blanket that was substituting for the crib of the Christ child.

The wise men, led by José Diaz, were

approaching from the left and the shepherds were gathering from the right.

'Slow down, all of you,' Sister Cordelia ordered. She raised, then lowered, her hands. 'One step at a time, and don't push. Jerry, keep your eyes *down*. You're supposed to be looking at the baby, not at the shepherds.'

'Willy, play the closing song,' she said.

'I left the sheet music home, Cordelia. I didn't think I'd be here this long.'

'Well, sing it then. God blessed you with a voice. Start to sing very low, the way you'll do when you're at the piano, then bring up the volume. The children will join in, starting with Stellina and Jerry, then the wise men and the shepherds, then finally the chorus.'

Willy knew better than to argue with his sister. 'Sleep, my child,' he began.

'José, I'll hang you out to dry if you trip Denny,' Sister Cordelia said, interrupting. 'Go ahead, start again, Willy.'

At 'Guardian angels God will send thee,' Stellina and Jerry joined in. Their young voices, sweet and true, combined with Willy's tenor as they sang the next two lines together.

What a beautiful voice that kid has, Willy thought as he listened to Stellina. I swear she has perfect pitch. He studied her solemn brown eyes. A seven-year-old shouldn't look so sad, he thought as the wise men and shepherds and then all the students joined in: 'Soft the drowsy hours are creeping, Hill and vale in slumber steeping, I my loving vigil keeping, All through the night.'

At the end, Willy, Sister Cordelia, Sister Maeve Marie and the assorted volunteer aides applauded vigorously. 'Just be this good two weeks from now at the actual performance, and we'll all be happy,' Cordelia told the children. 'Now put on your coats and hats and don't get them mixed up. Your folks will be here to collect you, and they shouldn't be kept waiting. They've been working all day and they're tired.' She turned to Willy. 'And I might add, so am I,' she said.

'It makes me feel good to know that even you have some limits,' Willy said. 'Okay, since I've been here this long, I may as well hang around and help you clean up.'

Twenty minutes later, he and the two nuns were at the door, waiting for Mrs. Nuñez to pick up Stellina and Jerry. When she arrived breathless and contrite, they waved away her apologies.

Sister Cordelia pulled her aside. 'How is Stellina's great-aunt doing?' she asked.

'Not good,' Mrs. Nuñez whispered, shaking her head. 'She'll be in the hospital before the week is out, is my guess.' She crossed herself quickly. 'Well, at least the father's back. That's something, I suppose.' She sniffed, as if to make it clear just how little faith she put in

Stellina's father.

When Mrs. Nuñez and the children had left, Sister Cordelia said, 'That poor child. Her mother deserted her when she was an infant. She's going to lose the great-aunt who raised her, and the father doesn't seem to he around much. From what I gather, he isn't worth a hill of beans.'

'He's worth less than that,' Sister Maeve Marie interjected. 'Friday evening, he tried to pick Stellina up after she was already gone. He looked a little unsavory to me, so I made some inquiries about him with the boys at the precinct.'

'Keeping your hand in at your old job, Detective?' Willy asked.

'It doesn't hurt. From the rumors, it sounds like Mr. Centino could be headed for big trouble.'

'Which means that lovely child could end up in a foster home, or a series of foster homes,' Sister Cordelia said sadly. 'And in a few weeks we won't be able even to watch out for her anymore.' She sighed. 'All right, enough. Go home, Willy. You've been great, and you can pick up your paycheck at the end of the week.'

'Very funny.' He smiled, acknowledging her customary joke. As they left the building, they stood together for a moment on the sidewalk. 'Have a glass of wine and relax, you two,' Willy said. 'I would take you out to dinner, but I haven't spoken to Alvirah since she called at noon to say she was going condo hunting, so I don't know when we'll be eating.'

Cordelia looked astonished. 'You're kidding. I thought you loved the place you're in. Why, Alvirah always said she'd have to be carried out of that apartment. Don't tell me she's serious about buying a different one.'

'Of course not,' Willy assured her. 'She's just trying to get a line on that real estate couple who witnessed Bessie signing the will. She's hoping that if she goes out enough with one or the other of them, she might find out there was something fishy about that witnessing. Anyhow, I'm on my way, but you girls have done a great job. That pageant is going to be terrific. You ought to invite the mayor—let him see what you're doing.'

The compliment did nothing to put cheer in their worried faces, and when he got home, an equally troubled Alvirah was waiting for him. 'I've walked my feet off looking at condos with Eileen Gordon,' she said.

'Learn anything?' Willy asked.

'Yes, she's a lovely person, and I'd stake my life she wouldn't take a sip of water that didn't belong to her, even if she was choking.'

'So that means the Bakers probably pulled the old one-two on her and her husband,' Willy said practically.

'Yes, but I was so hoping they'd turn out to

111

be phonies too. It's easier to trap crooks than to convince innocent bystanders that they've been duped,' Alvirah said with a sigh.

CHAPTER EIGHTEEN

Monsignor Thomas Ferris's association with St. Clement's had begun forty years earlier, when he was a newly ordained priest. After seven years, he had been transferred to a parish in the Bronx; following that, he was assigned to the cardinal's staff at the cathedral office. Ten years ago, he had returned to St. Clement's as pastor, and it was there that he hoped to spend the rest of his active life. He acknowledged to himself that St. Clement's was his heart home; he took great pride in the church—its history and its important position in the community. The only incident that had marred his tenure, and one that still bothered him seven years later, was the theft of Bishop Santori's chalice.

'I blame myself because it happened on my watch,' he would say to brother priests who knew how strongly he felt about the loss. 'There had been warnings about a string of church break-ins, but we just hadn't paid sufficient heed. Sure, we'd had the windows and doors alarmed, but it wasn't enough. We should have installed a motion detector. I talked about it but just never got around to it.'

And while the cabinet containing the bishop's chalice had been equipped with a silent alarm, it had proved useless in this situation. By the time the police had arrived, the thief and the chalice were gone.

The loss always hit Monsignor Tom especially hard at the Christmas season, because it was during Advent that the chalice had disappeared. And while he and the parishioners constantly prayed for its return, his prayers were especially fervent at this time of year.

Some saints are born and not made—Tom Ferris believed that. He always held that they are born with an inner goodness that makes its presence felt, no matter what the circumstance. He had met Bishop Santori near the end of the bishop's life, after he had retired from official duties. The bishop had lived at St. Clement's until his death.

The man had an aura of holiness about him, Ferris reflected; that same aura had surrounded Cardinal Cooke.

On Monday evening, as the monsignor began to lock up the church, he passed the confessional. The thief who stole the chalice *had* to have been hiding in there, he thought. If the diamond in the chalice had been what he was after, I can only pray that the cup itself wasn't tossed away into a garbage dump.

The monsignor actually didn't believe that the chalice had been destroyed. In fact, recently he had been struck with the fanciful notion that the theft had taken place because the chalice was needed elsewhere, that in exile from its home at St. Clement's, it was fulfilling a greater mission.

As he left the church and locked the door behind him, he found himself automatically looking across the street to see if the mysterious young woman was there again today. When he saw she wasn't, he experienced a moment of regret; he hoped she would be back. Many times he had had the experience of people hovering nearby, reluctant to unburden themselves to him, who then finally screwed up their courage and approached him. *'Monsignor, I need help,'* is how they usually began.

His housekeeper had left dinner for him in the oven. His curate was out for the evening, so Tom Ferris had the luxury of reading without interruption while he ate the simple meal and sipped a glass of wine. When he had finished, he dutifully rinsed the dishes and put them in the dishwasher, remembering with some amusement the old days when the pastor—usually known among his six or seven curates as 'the boss'—reigned as absolute monarch, and when the rectory came with a housekeeper who could cook like a dream and happily provided, and served, delicious meals, three times a day.

It was over coffee that the tranquil part of

his evening ended with a phone call from Alvirah. 'Monsignor Tom,' she said, 'I have a friend with a problem, and while I think I may have figured out a solution, I need to talk with you about it. You see, I'm writing a column about a young girl who, seven years ago, gave birth and left her newborn on the stoop of a rectory.' She paused. 'And I'm telling you this because it was your rectory.'

'Alvirah, that never happened!'

'Yes, it did, but you didn't know anything about it. I'm convinced that it really did happen. Anyway, the point is that my editor will feature the story on the first page, and since we've got to protect the identity of the mother, we want any calls to be directed to you, because, after all, it *was* your rectory. I'll offer a big reward for information about the baby. You just have to handle the calls that come in.'

'Alvirah, slow down.'

'I can't. This is the perfect time for this kind of story to come out. For one thing, people pay more attention to this kind of human-interest story at Christmas, and for another, the child just turned seven last week. I'm writing the piece right now, and I need to know if it's all right to use your name as intermediary.'

'I'd want to see what you've written first,' he said cautiously.

'Of course. We really appreciate your

cooperation, and I'm sorry to have to impose this way, but through the article and the reward we're sure to get a lot of attention. We're really hoping to locate the little girl, and we're hoping that if we don't say who the mother is, some do-gooder won't try to make an example of her and have her arrested for abandonment or child abuse. The point is, is it better if you don't know who she is?'

'Let me think about that,' he said.

'It's not a problem for me,' Alvirah said. 'I can claim journalistic privilege if I get questioned.'

There is a way that I can't be forced to reveal her identity, Ferris thought, but the seal of the confessional is not to be used as a convenience.

'Wait a minute, Alvirah. You said this happened just about exactly seven years ago. Are you talking about the night the chalice was stolen? Was *that* when the baby was left?'

'Yes, apparently it was. When the mother phoned the rectory, an old priest answered. She asked to speak with you, and he told her that the police were there because of some great excitement and that you were outside with them. She thought you'd found the baby already.'

He made up his mind. 'Write your story, Alvirah. I'm with you.'

Monsignor Ferris hung up the phone with a

117

sense of wonderment. Was it possible that whoever took the baby might have seen the thief leaving the church and be able to provide at last a clue to his identity? By helping this unfortunate mother, the monsignor might be able to also put to rest the nagging question of what happened to the chalice.

CHAPTER NINTEEN

Whenever she went into Bessie's room, there was no question in Kate Durkin's mind that something was slightly out of order, but just what it was still eluded her. Exasperated by the nagging sensation, she finally prayed to Saint Anthony for help in finding whatever it was whose whereabouts she couldn't recall. In the course of her prayer she did admit to him that usually she was asking him for help with something tangible, like her glasses or pocketbook or her one piece of 'good' jewelry, the tiny solitaire diamond in a Tiffany setting that had been her mother's engagement ring.

That time it had taken Saint Anthony two weeks to help her remember that she had hidden it in an empty aspirin bottle when she and Bessie had gone on a senior citizens' bus trip to Williamsburg.

'You see, Saint Anthony,' she explained as she placed primly folded underwear in an open box on the bed, I *do* think that Alvirah just may be right, and that there's a chance the Bakers managed to fool Bessie and cheat me out of this house. Of course, I'm not *sure* she's right, but I *am* worried, because every time I come in this room and look at that desk with Bessie's old typewriter, a warning bell goes off

119

in my head.'

Kate noticed a run in a pair of folded stockings. 'Poor Bessie,' she said aloud. 'Her eyes were going, but she wouldn't let me take her for new glasses. She said it was a waste of money to buy them when she probably wouldn't last until Christmas.'

Well, she was right, Kate thought with a sigh as she opened the next drawer and reached for the flannel nightgowns that had been Bessie's uniform sleepwear. 'My stars,' she murmured, 'poor Bessie, she must have put this one back without noticing she'd worn it.' She shook her head as she brushed at the streak of powder on the neckline of a pink flowered gown with lace at the collar. 'I'll wash it before I pack it,' she murmured. 'Bessie would have liked that.'

She shook her head. No, actually I'm not surprised she tried it, then took it off, she said to herself. She never liked the lace. She said it scratched her neck. What surprises me is that she put it on in the first place.

She still had the gown in her hand when a sound made her turn. Once again, Vic Baker was at the door, observing her. 'I'm preparing my sister's clothing to be sent to charity,' she said sharply. 'Unless you and your wife also claim her nightdresses.'

Without answering, Vic turned away. That man *frightens* me, Kate thought. There's something scary about him. I'll be glad to get

120

out of here.

That evening she went to the washing machine and was surprised to see that Bessie's pink-flowered nightgown was missing from the small pile of laundry she had gathered and left there.

I must be losing my mind, Kate thought. I could have sworn I'd brought it down. Oh well, I must have packed it. Now I'll have to go through all those darn boxes looking for it.

CHAPTER TWENTY

On Friday, December 11th, Alvirah's story about the baby left at the rectory door of St. Clement's seven years ago appeared on the front page of the *New York Globe*. Almost from the minute the paper hit the stands, the phone calls began to pour into the special number at the rectory that Monsignor Ferris had hastily had installed.

His longtime secretary answered the calls, announcing that she was recording every conversation, and passed on to Monsignor the ones that seemed most likely to warrant further consideration. When he called Alvirah on Monday morning, however, the monsignor sounded glum. 'Of the more than two hundred calls we've received so far, not one has any merit,' he said. 'Unfortunately, a lot of them have been from indignant people saying that they have no sympathy for anyone who left a newborn out in the cold, even if only for a few minutes.'

'Have the police been around?' Alvirah asked.

'The Administration for Children's Services came by, and the caseworker I talked to was none too happy, believe me. The one thing we can establish is that there's no record of an unknown infant girl being found dead or abandoned in New York City at that time.'

'I guess that's something,' Alvirah said with a sigh. 'I'm so disappointed this hasn't led somewhere. And I thought it was such a good idea.'

'So did I,' Monsignor Ferris said in agreement. 'How is the mother doing? Incidentally, I've already figured out that she must be that young woman who was around here so often last week.'

'But you still can answer honestly that you don't know who she is, can't you?' Alvirah asked with some concern. As usual, she was recording their conversation, just in case Monsignor said something that escaped her at first hearing.

'You don't have to turn off your mike, Alvirah. I don't know who she is, and I don't *want* to know. By the way, what is this I hear about you hunting for a co-op?'

'My feet are walked down to stumps,' Alvirah admitted. 'The Gordons are both nice people, but Monsignor Tom, I've got to tell you that while they may be fine at selling real estate, they are *not* the brightest things God ever put on earth. I swear they can take you into a pokey little dungeon and then tell you it's charming, and, you know, the crazy part is that they *believe* it. Then they get all excited when they tell you that instead of the million-two the owner is asking, you can pick it

124

up for only nine hundred thousand dollars.'

'Real estate people have to be enthusiastic about the places they show, Alvirah,' Monsignor Ferris said mildly. 'It's known in some circles as optimism.'

'In their case, try tunnel vision,' Alvirah responded. 'Anyhow, I'm off with Eileen to see a place that she says has a spectacular view of Central Park. I can hardly wait. After that I'm going to go visit Kate and try to cheer her up.'

'I wish you would. She keeps reading her copy of Bessie's will and finding a new way to get her feelings hurt. The latest is that Bessie's signature was written with such force that the pen almost went through the paper. "It's as if she couldn't *wait* to give her house to strangers," she said.'

* * *

After hanging up, Alvirah sat for twenty minutes, lost in thought. Finally she put on her coat and hat and walked out onto the terrace.

The wind blew against her face, and she shivered, even though she was warmly dressed. I'm a failure, she told herself. I thought I was doing Sondra a favor—now she's gotten her hopes up, and for nothing. She'll be even more heartbroken. Her grandfather and boyfriend will be arriving tomorrow, and she has to keep up appearances in front of them as well as

125

practice for the concert on the 23rd.

And I also gave Kate a smidgen of hope that I'd find some way to break this new will, but after looking at just about every empty co-op on the West Side, the only sure thing I came up with is that Jim and Eileen are nice people who must just *luck* into sales, because they sure don't listen when you tell them what you want to see.

*   *   *

'Nothing so far,' she admitted sadly to Kate, when she stopped by the townhouse. 'But as I always say, it ain't over till it's over.'

'Oh, Alvirah,' Kate said. 'I think it's over. What bothers me is that I feel as if I'm living on an emotional roller coaster. I keep thinking of Bessie on that last Monday when I left her sitting there, watching her shows—you know how much she enjoyed *One Life to Live* and *General Hospital*—and going on about them, talking a mile a minute, telling me all about each character, and how they were all the time doing these terrible things to each other. And all the time she was planning to do something terrible to me.'

*   *   *

That night Alvirah had one of her crime-

126

solving bouts of insomnia. At one in the morning she finally gave up, went out to the kitchen, made tea and rewound her tape from the beginning.

Hercule Poirot, she thought. *Think like him!*

At seven, when Willy came out of the bedroom rubbing his eyes, he found a triumphant sleuth. 'Willy, I may have a handle on this,' she announced with an excited smile. 'It starts with Bessie's signature on the will. You can't tell much from a copy. This morning I'm going to march myself right down to probate court and get a good look at the original. You never know what I might find.'

'If there's anything to find, you'll find it, honey,' Willy said, his voice still sleepy. 'My money's on you.'

CHAPTER TWENTY-ONE

He had been offered something big—a bigger job than he had ever been in on before, bigger even than the one he had done for the fake computer company. It wasn't his usual style, but Lenny decided to take the risk—one big payoff, and he'd be set for years. Besides, he had decided it was time to take off for Mexico, especially now that Star's mother was in town and was on the hunt for her.

The story in the *New York Globe* had really rattled him. It described everything about the way Star was left on the rectory stoop; all the details were there. Suppose one of the nosy neighbors in his apartment building started counting on their fingers and remembered that it had been exactly seven years ago that he had arrived with his infant daughter—that thought really bothered Lenny. And who knew? Someone might even remember the shabby blue stroller with the stain on the side.

There even had been a lot of talk about the case on some of the radio shows. Don Imus in particular had zeroed in on it. He had the police commissioner on his program, and the commissioner had said that if the person or persons who had taken the baby were found, they might be charged with kidnapping and face the possibility of a long prison term.

'When you find any valuable object that isn't yours, even if you don't know who the owner is, you're supposed to turn it in,' the commissioner said. 'That's the law. And what could be more valuable than a human infant?'

He and Imus had talked about the note, which had been quoted word for word in the article. 'The fact that the mother wanted a good home for her child doesn't mean just *any* home,' the commissioner had said. 'That child became a ward of the city when the mother gave it up, and speaking for the city, we want her back. I would hope if anyone has even a suspicion of who might have that child, he or she will call in *immediately*. I guarantee no one will know who made the call, and the reward will be given without publicity.'

Something else dawned on Lenny that Tuesday morning as he stirred sugar and hot milk into a cup of strong coffee he was taking to Lilly. His aunt's health was worse—she hardly had gotten out of bed the last few days—and he knew that if she went to the hospital and talked about Star to anybody, social workers probably would come to the apartment to check on her.

When he reached Lilly's bedroom, her eyes were closed, but she opened them when she heard his footsteps. 'Lenny, I don't feel good,' she said, 'but I know if I go to the doctor, they'll put me in the hospital. I want to be able to see Stellina be the Blessed Mother in the pageant, so I want to wait awhile to go. But when I *do* go in the hospital, I want you to let her stay with Gracie Nuñez till I get back. You promise?'

Lenny knew that the pageant was next Monday afternoon, the 21st; that was also the day of his big job. He also knew that there wasn't even a chance Lilly would be able to go to the pageant, but if she could hold off that long before going to the hospital, everything would be great for him. Once the job was done, he would *make* Lilly go to the hospital, and when she was securely out of the way, he and Star would be on the road, probably by midnight. She's my lucky star, Lenny thought, and I've got to keep her with me.

He placed the coffee cup carefully on the wobbly night table next to the bed. 'I'm going to take good care of you, Aunt Lilly,' he promised. 'It'll break Stellina's heart if you're not there to at least see her in that nice outfit you sewed for her. And I agree that when you do go to the hospital, it would be a good idea if she stays with Mrs. Nuñez until you come back. I have to work, and I don't want her to be here all alone.'

Lilly looked pathetically grateful. '*Grazie*, Lenny, *grazie*,' she murmured, patting his hand.

131

The white tunic and blue veil were on a hanger on the clothes tree next to the dresser. As Lenny looked over at them, a gust of wind from the slightly open window sent the veil fluttering, and he watched as it drifted to the right and touched the chalice on the bureau.

Another warning, Lenny thought. The fact that the police had been at St. Clement's seven years ago because of the theft from the church had been prominently mentioned in the *Globe* article. The history of the chalice, and even a picture of it, had been a featured story on another page of the paper.

Lenny would have liked to grab the chalice and get rid of it, but he knew he couldn't risk that. If it disappeared, then Lilly would cause a stink, and Star would tell all her friends.

No, the chalice had to be put on hold too. But only for now. When he and Star finally did take off, there was one thing he knew for sure: That chalice was going to end up at the bottom of the Rio Grande.

CHAPTER TWENTY-TWO

Sondra could no longer bear to read a newspaper or turn on the television or listen to the radio. Alvirah's story about the baby had set off a media furor that made her cringe with shame.

On Monday night she had fished in her suitcase and found the unopened bottle of sleeping pills the doctor had prescribed, for when she had one of her occasional bouts of insomnia. She never had taken even one of them, preferring to tough it out rather than yield to the temptation to use something she considered a crutch. But by Monday, she knew she had no choice. She simply had to have some sleep.

When she awoke at eight on Tuesday morning, however, her cheeks were wet with tears, and she remembered that in her vague, troubled dreams she had been weeping. Groggy and disoriented, she finally managed to sit up and tentatively put her feet over the side of the bed.

For several seconds, the hotel room seemed to spin around her, the flowered draperies blending with the striped fabric on the couch in a kaleidoscope of color. I would have been better off either to have stayed awake all night—or to have swallowed every pill in the bottle, she thought fleetingly. But then she shook her head. I'm not that much of a coward, she told herself.

A long, hot shower, with the water pelting her face and soaking her hair, helped to restore some sense of focus. She pulled on a terry-cloth robe, wrapped her hair in a towel and forced herself to order scrambled eggs and toast with the usual juice and coffee.

Granddad and Gary are arriving tonight, she reminded herself. If they see me like this, they'll keep asking what's wrong until I break down and tell them the whole story. I've got to practice well today. And I've got to practice especially well tomorrow, when Granddad will be listening. I've got to give the kind of performance that makes him feel that all the years of teaching me and sacrificing for me were worth it.

Sondra got up and walked to the window. Today is Tuesday the 15th of December, she thought, as she looked down at the street, already bustling with midtown traffic and pedestrians rushing to work.

'The concert is next Wednesday,' she said aloud. The day after that is Christmas Eve— that's when we're supposed to go back to Chicago, she thought. Only I'm not going. Instead, I'm going to ring the bell of St. Clement's rectory, something I should have

134

done seven years ago instead of running two blocks to a phone. I'm going to tell Monsignor Ferris that I'm the baby's mother, and then I'll ask him to call the police. I can't live with this guilt for one day longer.

CHAPTER TWENTY-THREE

At ten o'clock on Tuesday morning, Henry Brown, a clerk at the Surrogates Court on Chambers Street in lower Manhattan, looked up and said, 'Good morning,' to a determined-looking woman of about sixty, with red hair and a somewhat prominent jaw. A keen judge of human nature, Henry noted the smile lines around the woman's mouth and the crinkles around her eyes. He knew that these hinted at a pleasant disposition, and that the irritation he saw in her face probably was just of the moment.

He thought he had her pegged: She'd be a disgruntled relative who would want to examine the will of a relative who had cut her off.

He quickly learned he was right about the desire to see a will, but the woman was not a relative.

'My name is Alvirah Meehan,' Alvirah explained. 'It's my understanding that wills filed for probate are public documents and I have the right to examine a particular one if I choose.'

'That's quite right,' Henry said pleasantly. 'But of course it must be in the presence of a member of the staff.'

137

'I don't care if the whole city government is hanging over my shoulder,' Alvirah said brusquely, but then softened. After all, it was not the fault of this helpful clerk that the closer she got to seeing Bessie's actual will, the more steamed up she felt herself becoming.

Fifteen minutes later, Henry Brown positioned beside her, she was studying the document. 'That word again,' she muttered.

'I beg your pardon?'

'It's just that the word "pristine" sticks in my craw. You see, I would swear that the lady who wrote this will never used that word in her entire eighty-eight years.'

'Oh, you'd be astonished how literary some people get when they write their wills,' Henry said helpfully. 'Of course, they do come up with some lulus, mistakes like "irregardless" or "to reiterate again."' He paused, then added, 'I must say, though, that "pristine" is a new one. I've never seen that word used before.'

Alvirah had tuned out when she heard the dismaying opinion that it might be considered customary to put some unfamiliar and perhaps highfalutin words into a will. 'Now, what's this?' she asked. 'I mean, look at this last page. The will is already signed.'

'That's known as the attestation clause,' Henry explained. 'By the terms of New York State law, the witnesses must complete this page. It attests that they've witnessed the

138

signing of the will, and the testatrix, in this case, Mrs. Bessie Durkin Maher, must also sign it. In essence it's a reconfirmation of the witnessing of the will. Without it, the witnesses would have to appear in court at the time of the probate, and, of course, when wills have been standing for years, the witnesses may have moved or died.'

'Take a look at this,' Alvirah ordered, holding up two pieces of paper. 'Bessie's signature on the will and then on this—what did you call it?—attestation clause. See there? The ink is different. But they had to be signed at the same time, right?'

Henry Brown studied the two signatures. 'Definitely these are two different shades of blue ink,' he said. 'But perhaps your friend Bessie decided her signature on the will, which while totally legible, was written in rather light ink, so she simply changed pens. There's nothing illegal about that. The witnesses signed with the same pen,' he pointed out.

'One of Bessie's signatures is firm, the other wavy. It's also possible that she signed these papers at two different times,' Alvirah said.

'Oh, that would be illegal.'

'I couldn't agree more!'

'Well, if you're quite finished, Mrs. Meehan . . .' Henry did not complete the sentence.

Alvirah smiled at him. 'No, I'm not, I'm afraid. I can't tell you how grateful I am to you

139

for giving me all this time, but I know you don't want there to be a miscarriage of justice.'

Henry smiled politely. Anybody who gets cut out of a will screams miscarriage of justice, he thought philosophically.

'Look, Henry,' Alvirah continued. 'It's all right if I call you Henry, isn't it? You should just call me Alvirah.' Without waiting to see if Henry accepted this elevation of their acquaintance, Alvirah said, 'Bessie swears this was her last will. I swear this thing is a phony. Besides, where did Bessie get the know-how to type this attestation clause? Tell me that.'

'Well, she may have asked someone to type it for her, or someone may have given her a copy of the form,' Henry said patiently. 'Now, Mrs. Meehan, I mean, Alvirah—' he began.

'All right,' Alvirah said, interrupting him. 'I know it's not proof, but these signatures look different, and I say Bessie didn't sign these papers at the same time.' Briskly she gathered up her things. 'Okay, Henry, thank you,' she said, rushing out, a woman with a mission.

*   *   *

Aivirah went directly to the James and Eileen Gordon Real Estate Agency. She was scheduled to see yet another co-op, this one on Central Park West and described by Eileen Gordon as 'a steal at two million.'

140

In the course of pretending interest in the place and hearing Eileen once again exclaim about the beautiful view—even though the view was somewhat limited, since the apartment was on the second floor and looked directly into trees—Alvirah managed to turn the conversation to the signing of Bessie's will.

'Oh, yes, the dear sweet old girl signed both papers,' Eileen said, her round eyes opening wide as she smiled reminiscently. 'I'm sure of that. But she was obviously getting very tired. I think that's why the second signature was quite wavy on the line. If she changed pens, I didn't notice. The truth is I may have been just kind of looking around the room. That townhouse is in almost perfect condition. I mean, a few things, like the living room door, need fixing, but that's nothing. With the way prices are now, I could get three million for that house easily.'

For once I think you're right, Alvirah thought, as, thoroughly disheartened, she turned off the microphone in her sunburst pin.

CHAPTER TWENTY-FOUR

'That Lenny Centino is smarter than he looks,' undercover detective Roberto Pagano told his boss, Joe Tracy, on Wednesday night when they got together at a prearranged meeting place. 'Since that first time I met him, he hasn't once shot his mouth off about the deliveries he made for the so-called computer company—or anything else we could pin on him. If it hadn't been for a couple of beers loosening his tongue, I don't think he'd have said anything that first time.'

'And at the least a smart lawyer could get any charges knocked down,' Joe worried. 'That's why I keep my fingers crossed he doesn't back out of the setup on Monday night.'

'I don't think he will,' Pagano said reassuringly. 'If my hunch is right, Lenny is playing traveling music. I think he knows it's getting hot for dealers on the Upper West Side these days. He wants to make his killing Monday night, then I'll bet you he's long gone.'

'Long gone, maybe, but not to where he thinks he's going, I hope,' Tracy replied. 'Sure, if Lenny goes through with the job, we have him hands down. But suppose he gets nervous and disappears on us?' Which brought something else to Tracy's mind. 'He's been picking up his kid the last few afternoons at that Home Base center. How come he's becoming such a good daddy all of a sudden?'

'Maybe he just wants to make sure that she remembers him after he takes off,' Pagano said with a shrug. 'I can't imagine he would let himself get saddled with a seven year-old.'

'I guess we can count on that,' Tracy agreed.

CHAPTER TWENTY-FIVE

The final rehearsal for the pageant was scheduled for Friday afternoon, and Lenny had made it a point to attend, explaining to Sisters Cordelia and Maeve Marie that since he would be at work at four o'clock on Monday afternoon when the pageant would be performed, he didn't want to miss his only chance to see his daughter as the Blessed Mother.

With his best stab at an ingratiating smile, Lenny explained that Stellina's nonna was very, very sick, but that he would always be there to take care of his little girl. 'It's you and me against the world, right, Star?' he asked, stroking the hair that was tumbling onto her shoulders. 'I'll even have to learn how to brush that pretty mop of yours.' He smiled again at the nuns. 'Nonna can't clip the barrette so good anymore.'

The women nodded, their expressions frosty. Then Sister Cordelia turned from him and clapped her hands. 'Okay, children, take your places for the final rehearsal. Oh, there you are, Willy. I was afraid you'd forgotten us.'

Willy and Alvirah were coming up the stairs, Willy's face wreathed in a smile of resignation. 'Cordelia, it's a week till Christmas. Believe it or not I had some shopping to do.'

'And I have made my last outing with the Gordons,' Alvirah said. 'They practically threw me out today. They said they sensed that I wasn't ready to make a move right now, and they gave me the names of some of their competitors I could call in case I wanted to keep looking for a co-op for the rest of my life.'

'Then we must accept that the good Lord doesn't want us to be in business after January first,' Cordelia acknowledged. 'And you mustn't blame yourself, Alvirah. You haven't left one stone unturned to try to prove Bessie's will was a fake.' She turned briskly away. 'Now let's get started with the rehearsal.' Turning back to Alvirah, she lowered her voice and nodded her head almost imperceptibly toward Lenny. 'That fellow there is Stellina's father. Sit next to him. He's trying to make a good impression on us, so I know he'll talk to you. See what you make of him. I think he's up to no good.'

Sister Cordelia was right. Lenny *did* talk— straight through the rehearsal, only interrupting his tale of how he gave up a good job in the Midwest because he missed Star so much but couldn't take her away from his beloved aunt, to make noisy and oddly inappropriate exclamations on how cute the children were. In the course of his ramblings,

146

he told Alvirah about the pretty Irish girl he had married who had been Star's mother.

'Her name was Rose O'Grady. We used to love to dance together. I'd get the band to play "Sweet Rosie O'Grady" when we were out, and I'd sing it in her ear.'

'What happened to her?' Alvirah asked.

'It's something I don't tell many people. She got postpartum depression so bad we had to have her hospitalized. Then—' Here Lenny's voice broke, fading off. 'They didn't watch her carefully enough.' The last words were delivered in a dramatic whisper.

Suicide, Alvirah thought. 'Oh, I'm so sorry,' she said sincerely.

'Nonna told Star her mama was sick and had to go far away, and that we probably wouldn't hear from her ever again. I think we should have maybe told her straight out that her mama was dead, but Nonna keeps saying not yet,' Lenny explained, pleased to have gotten the scenario down so well.

There was one small glitch in the rehearsal when Rajid, the third wise man, dropped the jar that supposedly held the myrrh. 'It's all right, Rajid,' Sister Cordelia called as she saw tears gather in his eyes, and Sister Maeve Marie swooped in to pick up the pieces. 'It was just a little accident. No real problem. Keep going, all of you.'

Willy went to the piano. It was time for the

closing scene in the pageant. 'Sleep, my child, and peace attend thee.' He played and sang softly.

Stellina and Jerry looked up from their kneeling position beside the cradle, which was now in place. 'Guardian angels God will send thee,' they sang, their voices young and sweet and true.

'That's a nice song,' Lenny said. It reminds me—'

'Sshh!' Dear God, can't he shut up long enough to listen to his own child? Alvirah thought, now so irritated that if she had had duct tape handy she surely would have pasted it across his mouth. She noticed that Stellina's eyes had flickered over to him when he spoke, but then turned away, as though in embarrassment.

She's savvy enough to know her father's a creep, Alvirah thought. That poor child. She actually looks a little untidy today. Her hair is tangled; usually it's pulled back so neatly.

Untidy, but still beautiful, she thought: the curly dark-blond hair, almost waist length, the fair complexion and haunting brown eyes. Her expression is almost adult in its sadness, Alvirah thought. Why do some kids get such a bad break in life?

Lenny clapped loudly when the rehearsal was over. 'Great!' he shouted. 'Really great stuff! Star, your daddy's proud of you!'

148

Stellina blushed and turned away, averting her eyes. 'Your daddy's proud of you,' Jerry mimicked as he got to his feet. 'You're such a good little Blessed Mother, ha, ha, ha.'

'It's still not too late to get a new Saint Joseph,' Sister Cordelia warned the boy, thumping him on the head. 'Now remember to bring your costumes to school with you Monday, children. You'll get dressed here.'

'I'm going to pick up Star at school and take her home to put on her costume,' Lenny told Alvirah. 'Her nonna can't make it to the pageant, but she wants to see her dressed up. Then I'll have to go to work.'

Alvirah nodded, absentmindedly, her attention focused on Cordelia as she collected the gifts the wise men were to present. The foil-covered chocolates made a realistic offering of gold, she thought. The painted bowl Cordelia had brought from the convent for the frankincense made a pretty offering. I'll pick up another jar to replace the one Rajid dropped, she thought. Then she noticed Stellina take Cordelia's hand and lead the nun to the side.

'Telling secrets?' Lenny observed, a tone of alarm creeping into his voice.

'Oh, I doubt that,' Alvirah said quickly. I know Stellina has been asking Sister Cordelia and Sister Maeve Marie to pray for her nonna.'

149

'Oh, yeah,' Lenny said after a few moments. 'I guess that must be what she's doing.'

* * *

Gratified with the impression he thought he had made at the rehearsal, Lenny left with Stellina, explaining to everyone in earshot that he was taking her out for dinner. 'Now that Nonna can't be worrying about meals, I guess I gotta get me a cookbook,' was his parting comment.

On the way to McDonald's, he asked Star if she had been asking the sister to pray for Nonna when she took the nun aside.

'I ask Sister that every day,' Stellina said quietly. Instinctively she knew that Daddy might not like what she had *really* asked Sister—that if Nonna allowed her to bring the silver chalice that had once belonged to her mother's uncle, could Rajid carry it to the stable, to replace the jar he broke?

To her delight, Sister had said that would be fine. Star was sure if she begged Nonna, she would give her permission to bring it. And when Rajid puts it down by the cradle, I will pray that if my mother hasn't gone to heaven yet, she will come to see me just once.

It was a wish and a hope that now had become almost a constant, urgent need. But a faith that was growing stronger and stronger seemed to promise Star that if the chalice could become a gift to the Christ child, her prayer would be answered.

Her mother really would come to her, at last.

CHAPTER TWENTY-SIX

Peter Lewis, Sondra's grandfather, arrived on Wednesday afternoon. It was both a relief and a disappointment to her that Gary did not accompany him. 'He'll be here for the concert,' her grandfather said, 'but he's very busy and could not take the extra time. Besides, I think he is astute enough to know that in the days before an artist is performing in a major concert, she is better left alone with her music, and with as few distractions as possible.'

Sondra knew what her grandfather was implying. Gary Willis loved music with a deep passion and understood the strains inherent I an artist's life.

'I'm glad he waited,' she said, 'but I'm thrilled that you're here. Granddad, you look spectacular.' It was an unexpected delight to her that her grandfather looked so well. Even though the signs of the arthritis were always visible in his swollen wrists and fingers, the triple bypass had restored color to his face and vigor to his appearance—things she had feared he had lost with age and illness.

When she told him how healthy he looked for his years, he responded, 'Thanks, Sondra, but seventy-five is considered to be only the dawn of aging today. An unobstructed blood supply to the heart does wonders, although I hope that's something you never need to find out for yourself.'

At least, Sondra thought, in an effort to draw some comfort from the situation, Granddad looks strong enough to take it when I tell him about the baby and what I'm going to do after the concert. But just thinking about it, she grew paler.

'And you look thin and troubled,' he told her crisply. 'Is something wrong, or is it just the usual preperformance nerves? If so, I'm disappointed. I thought I had cured you of that.'

She had turned aside the question. 'Granddad, this *is* Carnegie Hall,' she had told him. 'It's different.'

He had then spent Thursday and Friday renewing old friendships, while she practiced with her New York coach.

On Friday evening, at dinner, he talked about his visit to St. Clement's and having learned of the theft of Bishop Santori's chalice. 'Apparently that same night a baby was abandoned there.' he said as he studied the menu, absorbed as always in the task at hand. 'It seems to have been the subject of a recent newspaper article.' He paused. 'Grilled Dover sole and a salad,' he announced, then he looked across the table at her, his eyes probing. 'When I take you to Le Cirque 2000,

154

my dear, at least have the courtesy to look interested in the menu.'

The next day, when he came to hear her practice, she could read the disappointment in his eyes. She was rehearsing a Beethoven sonata, and while she knew her playing was technically perfect, she was also aware that there was neither passion nor fire in her music. And she knew that her granddad was aware as well.

When she was finished, he shrugged. 'Your technique is marvelous; it can't be faulted. But you have always withheld something of yourself from your music. Why, I don't know. Now you are withholding *everything*.' He looked at her sternly. 'Sondra, keep it up, and you will appear and immediately disappear from the major concert stage, like *that!*' He snapped his fingers. 'What is wrong? You withhold yourself from a man who loves you, and whom I believe you love in return. You resent me. I do not know why, but I have been aware of it for years. Does nothing touch you?'

With a shrug of dismay and resignation, he turned and began walking toward the studio exit.

'I am the mother of the baby who was abandoned at St. Clement's,' she shouted at him, the words hanging in the air.

He stopped and turned, his expression incredulous, but with a look of deep concern in his eyes.

With little expression in either her face or her voice, Sondra told him everything, the words rushing out of her.

When she was finished, there was a long silence. Then he nodded. 'So that is it. And I see that, in a way, you blame me because you let her go. Maybe you are right and maybe you are not. It is no matter. We will move heaven and earth to find her. We will tell Gary; he has enormous resources at his disposal. And if he does not understand, then he is not worthy of you. Now,' he picked up Sondra's violin and thrust it into her hands. 'Now play with all your heart to the child you are seeking.'

Sondra tucked the violin under her chin and reached for her bow. In her mind she could see her child. But would she have blond hair like her own, or would it be like her father's—silky, dark? Her eyes—were they still blue or brown like hers, or dark hazel like his? He was a man she had known so briefly, and in the end cared not a whit about, but he had fathered her child. She will be like me, Sondra decided. She will look as I did at her age.

She's seven now; music must be in her soul, she reflected as she drew the bow across the strings. She still eludes me, but I see her in the distance. I hear her footsteps. I feel her presence. She senses that I want her. Forgetting her grandfather, Sondra began to play.

156

I never gave her a name, she thought. What would I have called her? What do I call her in my heart? She sought the answer as she played, but could not find it.

When the last notes faded into silence, after a long pause, her grandfather nodded. 'Now you are becoming a true musician. You are still holding back, but that was an infinite improvement. You will be required to play an encore. What have you chosen?'

Sondra did not know what her answer would be until she heard herself say it: 'A simple song of Christmas,' she told him. "All Through the Night."'

CHAPTER TWENTY-SEVEN

On Sunday morning Alvirah and Willy went to Mass at St. Clement's. Kate Durkin was in attendance as well, and, at her insistence, they went back to the townhouse for coffee.

When they arrived, the Bakers were just going out. 'Linda and I are on our way to pick up the morning papers,' Vic said jovially. 'We always take a crack at the Sunday *Times* puzzle.'

'I knew a guy who claimed to ace it every week, but when somebody checked him once, they found he was cheating, putting down gobbledygook to fill in the blanks,' Willy said. 'A friend of yours maybe?'

Baker's smile froze. Linda shrugged and tugged at his sleeve. 'Come on, hon,' she pleaded.

'I see he put away his black tie,' Willy observed, as he watched them walk down the block arm in arm.

'It's a wonder she doesn't break her neck in those high heels,' Alvirah observed. 'There are patches of ice all over the sidewalk.'

'Trust me, she won't fall,' Kate said. 'She's a pro in those things—wears them all the time.' Kate turned the key in the lock and pushed open the door. 'Come on in. That wind goes right through you.'

'Let's have our coffee in the parlor,' she said as they took off their coats. 'I lit the fire in there this morning, and it feels cozy. Bessie loved to sit in the parlor and have coffee and my fresh-baked crumb cake after Mass on Sundays.'

Kate refused to allow Alvirah to assist her in setting things out. 'What's a few cups and plates! You've been running around on my behalf all week. Go in and sit down.'

'I always liked this room,' Willy observed as he settled into the deep leather chair that had been the treasured possession of Judge Aloysius Maher, whose portrait in judicial robes still looked down at them benignly from the wall over the mantel.

'It's a wonderful room,' Alvirah agreed. 'You don't get these high ceilings and carved mantels anymore. just look at the details on the windows. That's workmanship. I can't stand it that poor Kate isn't going to get to enjoy all this for the rest of her life.' She turned around, then sighed. 'Well I guess Bessie won't mind if I take her favorite chair. I can just see her sitting here, her feet on the hassock, watching her shows—and woe betide you if you interrupted her during *One Life to Live* or *General Hospital*. Then what does she do with her next-to-last breath? She sneaks upstairs when Kate's back is turned, and just to

160

do her out of this house. Why, that means she missed at least one of her shows on her very last day on earth.'

'Maybe they have *Soap Opera Digest* in heaven, and she's been able to catch up,' Willy suggested.

Kate came in carrying a tray, which she placed on the coffee table. 'Oh, Willy,' she said, 'would you mind closing the door. "Hon" and "Dearie" will be back with the papers any time now, and I don't want them to come in and bother us.'

'My pleasure, Kate,' Willy said with a grunt as he got up.

At the mention of the Bakers, the subject of the will came up. As a reflex gesture, Alvirah turned on the microphone in her sunburst pin.

'Bessie always wrote with the judge's pen, and she never used blue ink in it,' Kate said when Alvirah talked about the differing shades of blue ink on the will and the attestation clause. 'But then again, she did a lot of crazy things during those last few days.'

'What about her typewriter?' Alvirah asked. I thought she said something about it on Thanksgiving.'

'I'm not sure,' Kate murmured.

'All right. How bad was her eyesight?' Alvirah queried.

'She had bifocals; you know that. But the prescription for the reading lenses needed to

161

be strengthened. If she didn't hold something up close to her face, she had trouble making it out. She may have signed those papers thinking she was signing for a delivery of paint or varnish or tools,' Alvirah said. 'I was here once when Baker brought her a receipt to sign for a delivery. He handed her his pen.'

'All of which won't help you in court,' Willy observed. 'Kate, I'd walk a mile for a piece of that crumb cake.'

Kate smiled. 'No need to do that—there's plenty right here. Bessie loved it too. Told me that even after she was gone, I should fix a piece for her and set it out in this room on Sunday mornings. She said she'd haunt me if I forgot.'

And then along came the Bakers, Alvirah thought. From the foyer she heard the click of the outside door. 'The heirs are back,' she murmured, and then watched in dismay as the door to the parlor swung open and Vic and Linda Baker smiled in on them.

'Elevensies,' Vic said in his usual jovial tone. 'That's what they call it in England, having a morning snack break like this. It's always around eleven o'clock.' He took a step into the room. 'My, that crumb cake looks spectacular, Kate.'

'It is,' Alvirah said flatly. 'Didn't you adjust that door for Bessie, Mr. Baker?'

'As a matter of fact, I did, yes.'

162

'Is that why it swings open so easily?'

'It needs a bit more adjusting.' Clearly uncomfortable with the conversation, he turned to leave. 'Well, I'm off to try my hand at the puzzle.'

They waited until the sound of Vic's heavy footsteps and the bouncy staccato of Linda's heels could no longer be heard. 'You can't insult that guy, can you?' Willy observed.

'It's more than that,' Kate said. 'He's curious about what we're saying. Thank God, I'm almost through clearing out Bessie's room. He always hangs around when I'm in there.' She frowned. 'You know, Alvirah, talking about the typewriter, the space bar has needed fixing too. Unless you type very slowly, it keeps skipping. That just dawned on me. I've been looking at the typewriter there in Bessie's room, trying to remember what Bessie *did* say on Thanksgiving.'

Alvirah swallowed the last drop of coffee and regretfully declined a second piece of crumb cake. 'Let me take a look at that typewriter,' she said.

There were a few sheets of plain paper in Bessie's desk. Alvirah inserted one into the typewriter carriage and began to type. The carriage skipped several spaces whenever she touched the space bar, forcing her to use the back key constantly. 'How long has it been like this?'

'At least since Thanksgiving.'

'Meaning either Bessie typed her will *before* Thanksgiving—which would have meant that she was lying in her teeth to Monsignor when he saw her the day after Thanksgiving—or she typed it over the weekend, literally one word at a time. Who's kidding who?'

'But it doesn't add up to proof, honey,' Willy reminded her. He looked at the stack of boxes against the wall in Bessie's room. 'Kate, can I help you with those?'

'Not yet. There's one more thing to pack up, and I can't find it. I put a pink-flowered flannel gown of Bessie's out to wash, and now it's disappeared. It had a streak of face powder on it, and I don't want to let it go out soiled.' She lowered her voice and looked furtively over her shoulder. 'You know, if Linda Baker didn't dress like a dime-a-dance girl, I'd swear Vic might have taken it for her. Now what do you make of *that?*'

*   *   *

That afternoon, while Willy watched the Giants play the Steelers, Alvirah sat at the dining room table and once again listened to all the taped conversations she had collected concerning Bessie's will and the townhouse. As she listened she made notes, her brow furrowing as certain remarks jumped out

164

at her.

The score was tied, and the game was in the fourth quarter when she yelled, 'I think I figured it out! Willy, Willy, listen to me. Would you have called Bessie a "dear, sweet old girl"?'

Willy did not take his eyes off the screen. 'No. Never. Not on the best day of her life.'

'Of course not. Because she *wasn't* a dear, sweet old girl. She was a tough, stubborn, crusty old girl. But that's what it's all about. And after all that trooping around I did with the Gordons, I finally figure it out sitting right here at home!'

Even though the Giants had made a first down and were on the Steelers' three-yard line, Willy gave Alvirah his full attention. 'What did you figure out, honey?'

'The Gordons never laid eyes on Bessie,' Alvirah said triumphantly. 'They witnessed somebody else signing that will. Vic and Linda sneaked in a ringer while Bessie was watching her shows.'

*   *   *

Two hours later, Alvirah and Willy arrived at Kate's townhouse with Jim and Eileen Gordon in tow. They already had alerted Monsignor Ferris and Sisters Cordelia and Maeve Marie to be there, and they found them sitting in the

165

parlor with an equally bewildered Kate.

'Alvirah, what's all this about?' Cordelia demanded.

'You'll see. The heirs are joining us, aren't they?' Alvirah asked.

'The Bakers?' Kate replied. 'Yes, I told them you were coming, and that you said you'd have a surprise for them.'

'Wonderful. Kate, you haven't met these nice people have you? Jim and Eileen Gordon witnessed—or *thought* they witnessed—Bessie signing the will.'

'*Thought* they witnessed?' the monsignor said.

'Exactly. Now, Eileen, you tell us what happened when you came in that day,' Alvirah said.

Eileen Gordon, an earnest expression on her pleasant face, said, 'Well, if you remember, we had been out with Mr. Baker, showing him a simply beautiful duplex on West Eighty-first, right across from the museum. It's in one of the finest buildings in the—'

'Eileen,' Alvirah said, struggling to control her irritation, 'tell us about witnessing the will.'

'Oh, yes, well, Mrs. Baker had called, and when we arrived here with Mr. Baker, Mrs. Baker asked us to come in quietly. She said there was an elderly lady in the parlor who didn't like to be disturbed when she was watching her programs. The door was shut, so

166

we tiptoed up the stairs to the bedroom, where Mrs. Maher was waiting for us.'

'Elderly lady in the parlor!' Kate exploded. 'That was Bessie!'

'Then who was in the bedroom?' Monsignor Ferris asked.

The Bakers were heard coming down the stairs. 'Why don't we ask Vic?' Alvirah suggested as the couple entered the parlor. 'Vic, who was the lady you dressed up in Bessie's pink-flowered nightgown? An actress? Another cheat who was in on the deal?' Baker opened his mouth to speak, but Alvirah didn't give him a chance. 'I have plctures of Bessie that we took here just a few weeks ago, at Thanksgiving—nice, clear close-ups.' She handed the photos to the Gordons. 'Tell them what you told me.'

'She is definitely not the lady who was in bed and who signed that will,' Jim Gordon said, looking at the photos.

'Yes, there was a similarity, but no way is this the lady,' Eileen Gordon agreed as she vigorously shook her head.

'Tell us the rest, Eileen,' Alvirah suggested.

'When we came downstairs the door to the parlor had swung open, and we could see an old lady sitting in that chair.' Eileen pointed to Bessie's chair. 'She didn't turn her head, but I could see her profile—*she* was definitely the lady in Alvirah's Thanksgiving pictures.'

'How much more do you need to hear, Vic, old boy?' Willy asked. 'Tomorrow morning, Kate files to contest the will, the Gordons tell their story and I give it a few days before you frauds are indicted.'

'I think it's time for us to move on,' Vic Baker said pleasantly but quickly. 'Kate, because of this misunderstanding, we'll be leaving immediately. Come, Linda. We'll pack right away.'

'Good riddance to the two of you. I hope you go to jail,' Alvirah called after them.

*   *   *

'You told me to bring champagne,' Monsignor Ferris said to Alvirah a few minutes later as they stood in the dining room and he popped the cork on the bottle. 'I see why.'

Sister Cordelia and Kate were both just beginning to understand what all this meant. 'Now I'll never have to leave my home,' Kate gasped.

'And I won't have to abandon my kids,' Sister Cordelia exulted. 'Praise be to God.'

'And to Alvirah,' Sister Maeve Marie said, holding up her glass.

For a moment a shadow came across Monsignor Ferris's face. 'Now if only you could set things right for that missing baby and retrieve the bishop's stolen chalice, Alvirah.'

'As Alvirah always says, "It ain't over till it's over," ' Willy said proudly. 'And as I always say, my money's on her.'

CHAPTER TWENTY-EIGHT

As promised, on Monday afternoon, Lenny picked up Stellina at her school. 'Star,' he said hurriedly, 'Nonna just had a weak spell, and the doctor came. They're sending for an ambulance. She may have to be in the hospital for a while, but she'll be fine. I promise you.'

'Are you sure?' Stellina asked, looking searchingly into his eyes.

'You bet.'

Stellina ran ahead, and as she turned the corner she saw a stretcher being wheeled from their apartment house along the sidewalk to a waiting ambulance. Her heart pounding, she raced to it.

'Nonna, Nonna,' she cried, reaching for her beloved great-aunt.

Lilly Maldonado tried to smile. 'Stellina, my heart is not so good, but they'll make it better, and then I'll be back. Now you must wash your hands and face, and brush your hair, and put on your Blessed Mother outfit. You can't be late for the pageant. Then tonight, after the pageant, Daddy will bring some of your clothes to Mrs. Nuñez's; you'll sleep at her house till I get back.'

Stellina whispered, 'Nonna, Rajid, who is one of the wise men, broke the jar that was

171

supposed to hold the myrrh. May I please, please bring my mother's cup for him to carry in the pageant? It was a holy cup. You told me it belonged to her uncle, a priest. Please. I'll take such good care of it. I promise.'

'We have to go, little girl,' the ambulance attendant said, tugging at Stellina's arm, trying to get her away from the stretcher. 'You can visit Nonna at St. Luke's Hospital. It's on 113th Street, not far from here.'

Tears came to Stellina's eyes. 'I have a prayer that I just know will come true if I bring my cup, Nonna. Please say it's okay.'

'What is your prayer, *bambina*?' Lilly's voice was heavy as the sedation the emergency crew had administered began to take effect.

'That my mother will come back,' the little girl said, tears starting to roll down her cheeks.

'Ah, Stellina, *bambina*, if only she would come before I die. Yes, yes, take the cup, but don't let Daddy see you. He might not let it go.'

'Oh, Nonna, thank you. I'll come and see you tomorrow, I promise.'

Moments later, the ambulance, its siren shrieking, was gone.

'Star, we've got to hurry,' Lenny urged.

*   *   *

Home Base was festively decorated with a
172

Christmas tree and beribboned ropes of pine. Over the weekend, some volunteers had built a platform at one end of the big upstairs room to give the effect of a stage. Another volunteer had hung ancient velvet portieres at both sides of the platform. Folding chairs had been set up for the audience, and the parents and siblings and friends of the children in the pageant were now happily pouring into the room.

Alvirah had arrived early to help Cordelia and Maeve get the children dressed for the pageant. By means of dire threats, Sister Cordelia was able to maintain reasonable order among the excited performers. At ten of four, just as they were all getting nervous about her, Stellina arrived.

Alvirah quickly took her in hand. 'Did your nonna see you in your outfit?' she asked as she straightened the blue veil over Stellina's waterfall of dark-gold hair.

'No. They took her to the hospital in an ambulance,' Stellina said quietly. 'Daddy promised to take me to see her. Will she get better, Mrs. Meehan?'

'Oh, I hope so, dear. But we will help take care of you while she's away. You know how afraid we were that we would have to close Home Base? Well, now, because of a miracle, we can keep it open—and that means we'll see you every day after school.'

Stellina's smile was wistful. 'Oh, I'm very

glad. I'm happy here.'

'Now run over there and take your place with Saint Joseph. Can I hold that bag for you?' Alvirah reached to take the plastic grocery bag Stellina was clutching.

'No, thank you. I have to give my cup to Rajid to carry. Sister Cordelia said it was all right for me to bring it. Thank you, Mrs. Meehan.'

As she scurried to where the other children were gathered, Alvirah stared after her. What is it about that child? She reminds me of someone—but who? she asked herself as she went to her seat.

The lights dimmed. It was time for the Christmas pageant to begin.

*   *   *

'Simply wonderful!' was the universal comment as the last notes of 'All Through the Night' faded away and the applause began. Cameras flashed from all around the room as parents acted to preserve the moment. Alvirah suddenly tugged at Sister Maeve Marie's sleeve. 'Maeve, I want you to get a close-up of Stellina,' she said. I mean *several* close-ups of her.'

'Sure, Alvirah,' Maeve agreed. 'She was the perfect Blessed Mother. When she sang, she brought tears to my eyes. She put so much

174

feeling into the words.'

'Yes, she did. She has music in her soul.'

A wild, crazy thought that was becoming certainty had crept into Alvirah's head, but she didn't want to admit it even to herself. We can try to check the birth records for a start, she thought, but oh, dear God, is it possible?

'I've got some good ones of her,' Maeve said a few minutes later, gingerly holding out the Polaroid photos she had taken. 'They'll be clearer once they finish developing. And I have a cute one of her and Rajid. He's handing her silver cup back to her.'

Her silver cup? No! *Her chalice!* Alvirah thought. You may he wrong, she warned herself. You could be just getting carried away. But one thing at least can be proved immediately. 'Maeve, if you've got more film, get some close-ups of that cup,' she said. 'Ask Stellina to hold it up for you.'

'Alvirah, come on,' Willy called. 'You're supposed to hand me the presents to give the kids.'

'Maeve, get those close-ups and hang on to them for me,' Alvirah ordered. 'Don't let them out of your hands.'

She hurried to Willy's side. The presents were on a table behind her. 'All right, Santa, this is for José,' she announced heartily, as the young boy eagerly reached out his hands.

Willy put an arm around him. 'Wait a

175

minute, José. Sister Maeve will be right over to take a picture of us.'

Alvirah was frantic to get away, to be off following up on her suspicions, but it was easier just to finish helping Willy with the presents than to get someone else to do it.

Meanwhile, Cordelia and her volunteers were busy passing out candy and soda, although some people had begun to leave. To Alvirah's dismay, she saw that Grace Nuñez was about to depart with José and Stellina in tow.

When she called out to her, Grace bustled over. 'Where are you taking Stellina?' Alvirah asked.

'I'm gonna drop her off at home for now,' Grace explained. 'Her daddy will bring her to stay with me tonight. He says he wants to have dinner with her first, after he gets off work. I got to stop at my sister's for a while, but he told me he'll be home early. She knows to lock the door herself, don't you, Stellina?'

'Yes, I do. Oh, I hope he'll be able to tell me how Nonna is,' Stellina said earnestly.

Ten minutes later all the presents had been dispensed and all the pictures taken. Alvirah ran to Sister Maeve Marie and picked up the Polaroid shots. Then she grabbed her coat.

'What's up?' Willy asked, his voice muffled through his fuzzy Santa Claus beard.

'I've got to show Monsignor Tom some

pictures,' she said over her shoulder. 'Meet me there.'

* * *

The monsignor was out but was expected back soon, Alvirah was told. Willing the time to pass quickly, she waited in the rectory parlor, pacing back and forth. Willy and the monsignor arrived at the same time, half an hour later. The monsignor was smiling. 'What a nice surprise, Alvirah,' he said cheerfully.

Alvirah didn't waste words. She handed him the pictures. 'Monsignor Tom, look at these.'

He studied the picture of Stellina taking the cup from Rajid during the pageant, then he looked at the close-up Maeve Marie had made of the cup alone.

'Alvirah,' he said quietly, 'do you know what this is?'

'I think so. It's Bishop Santori's chalice. And do you know who I think that little girl is?'

He waited.

'I think she's the infant who was left at your rectory door the night the chalice was stolen.'

CHAPTER TWENTY-NINE

Grace Nuñez walked Stellina to the door of the apartment she shared with Nonna and her daddy. She watched like a mother hen while the little girl went in, then listened for her to turn the double lock. 'I'll see you later, honey,' she called from the hallway, then left, confident that Stellina would never open the door to anyone except her father.

Inside the apartment it was quiet and dark; Stellina noticed the difference immediately. Without Nonna, it seemed strange and lonely. She went around the apartment turning on lights, hoping to brighten the place. Going into Nonna's room, she started to take off her Blessed Mother costume, but then stopped. Nonna had wanted to see her wearing it, and she hoped that her daddy would take her to the hospital.

She took the silver cup out of the bag and sat on the edge of the bed. Holding the cup made her feel less alone. Nonna had never before been away when she came home, never once.

*　　　*　　　*

At seven o'clock, Stellina heard footsteps

pounding up the stairs to the hallway. It couldn't be Daddy, she thought. He never runs.

But then he was banging on the door. 'Star, open up! Open up!' he cried frantically.

As soon as he heard the click of the locks, Lenny turned the handle and threw himself into the apartment. It had been a setup! The whole thing had been a trap! He should have *known* it, he told himself, snarling. That lousy new guy in the crew was an undercover cop. Lenny had managed to get away by the skin of his teeth once he realized what was going on, but they were no doubt combing Fort Lee for him right now, and they would be checking this place in minutes. He had to risk stopping here, though—his fake identity papers and all his cash were in the bag he had packed and left here this afternoon.

He raced into his room and grabbed the bag from under his bed. Stellina followed him and stood in the doorway, watching. Lenny turned to glance at her and saw that she was holding the chalice. Well, that was good, he thought. He wanted it out of here, and the sooner the better.

'Come on, Star, let's go,' he ordered. 'We're getting outta here. Don't try to bring anything but your cup.' He knew he probably was crazy to bring the kid now that the police were after him, but she was his good-luck charm—his lucky star.

'Will you take me to see Nonna, Daddy?'

'Later, maybe tomorrow. I told you, come on. We got to go.' He grabbed her hand and headed back down the hall, pulling her behind him.

Stellina grasped her silver cup as she stumbled to keep up with his pace. Without locking the door behind them, they raced down the stairs—one flight, two flights, three flights, as she struggled not to fall.

At the last landing before the lobby, Lenny stopped abruptly and stood listening. Nothing so far, he thought, feeling a moment of relief. He only needed another minute and they would be in the car he had managed to steal, and then he was home free.

He was halfway across the foyer when the outer door suddenly burst open. Yanking Star in front of him, Lenny pretended to reach for a gun. 'You shoot me and she gets it,' he shouted, without conviction.

Joe Tracy was at the head of the squad. He wasn't about to risk a child's life, however hollow the threat. 'Everybody back!' he ordered cautiously. 'Let him go.'

The car Lenny had was only a few feet from the front of the building. The police watched, helpless, as he dragged Star to the vehicle, opened the driver's door and threw in his bag. 'Get in and crawl over to the other side,' he told her urgently. He knew he would never hurt her, but hopefully the cops didn't.

Star obeyed, but when Lenny got in and slammed his door, he let go of her hand to turn on the ignition key. In a lightning moment, she opened the passenger door and jumped out of the car. Clutching the chalice, her veil flying behind her, she ran down the street as the police closed in on the car.

*   *   *

Ten minutes later, Alvirah, Willy and Monsignor Ferris arrived to find Lenny handcuffed and seated in a patrol car. They climbed the stairs to the apartment and learned that Stellina and the chalice were missing.

As they stood in the living room of the apartment where Stellina had lived these past seven years, they told Joe Tracy about the chalice, and about their suspicion that Stellina was the missing infant of St. Clement's.

One of the policemen came in from Lenny's bedroom. 'Take a look at this, Joe. Found it wedged between the shelf and wall in the closet.'

Joe read the crumpled note, then handed it to Alvirah. 'She *is* the missing infant, Mrs. Meehan,' he said. 'This confirms it. It's the note the mother pinned to her blanket.'

'I have a call to make,' Alvirah said with a sigh of relief. 'But I don't want to make it until Stellina is found . . .'

'We're combing the city for her,' Tracy said as his cell phone rang. He listened for a moment, then broke into a broad smile. 'You can go ahead and make your call,' he told Alvirah. 'The little Blessed Mother was just picked up attempting to walk all the way to St. Luke's Hospital to see her nonna.' He spoke into his phone. 'Take her over there,' he ordered. 'We'll meet you at the hospital.' He turned to Alvirah, who had picked up the phone that sat on an end table. 'I presume you're trying to get in touch with the child's mother.'

'Yes, I am.' Let Sondra be in the hotel, Alvirah prayed.

'Ms. Lewis left a message that she is having dinner in the restaurant with her grandfather,' the desk clerk said. 'Shall I page her?'

When Sondra came on the line, Alvirah said, 'As fast as you can, grab a cab and get up to St. Luke's Hospital.'

Detective Tracy took the phone from her. 'Forget the cab. I'm sending a squad car for you, ma'am. There's a little girl I'm sure you'll want to see.'

*   *   *

Forty minutes later, Alvirah, Willy, Monsignor Ferris and Joe Tracy met Sondra and her grandfather outside Lilly's room in the hospital's cardiac care unit.

'She's in there with the woman who has raised her,' Alvirah whispered. 'We haven't told her about anything. That's for you to do.'

White faced and trembling, Sondra pushed open the door.

Stellina was standing at the foot of the bed, her profile to them. The soft light seemed to halo the shining gold hair that spilled from beneath the blue veil.

'Nonna, I'm glad you're awake now, and I'm so glad you feel better,' she was saying. 'A nice policeman brought me here. I wanted you to see me in my beautiful dress. And see, I took very good care of my mother's cup.' She held up the silver chalice. 'We used it in the pageant, and I made my prayer—that my mother would come back. Do you think that God will send her to me?'

With a sob, Sondra crossed to her daughter's side, knelt down and folded her in her arms.

In the hallway, Alvirah pulled the door closed. 'There are some moments that aren't meant to be shared,' she said firmly. 'Sometimes it's enough just to know that if you believe hard enough and long enough, your wishes can come true.'

EPILOGUE

Two nights later, on December 23rd, a capacity audience gathered at Carnegie Hall for the gala concert that would feature luminaries of the musical world and would be the New York debut for the brilliant young violinist Sondra Lewis.

In a prime center box, Alvirah and Willy were seated with Stellina; Sondra's grandfather; her boyfriend, Gary Willis; Monsignor Ferris; Sister Cordelia; Sister Maeve Marie and Kate Durkin.

Stellina, the object of countless curious glances, was seated right in the front row, her brown eyes sparkling with delight, blissfully unaware of the stir she was causing.

For two days the city newspapers had featured the story of the reunited mother and child and the recovery of the beloved chalice. It was a wonderful human-interest story and especially appropriate for the Christmas season.

The articles had featured pictures of Sondra and Stellina, and as Alvirah said, 'Even a blind man could see Stellina's a clone of her mother. I can't believe it didn't hit me sooner.'

When questioned about indicting Sondra for abandonment, the district attorney had said, 'It would take a bigger Scrooge than even my enemies think I am to press charges against that young woman. Did she make an error by not ringing the bell of the rectory instead of running to a phone? Yes, she did. Did she, an eighteen-year-old kid, do her best to find a home for her baby? You bet she did.'

To which the mayor had responded, 'If he *had* indicted her, I'd have made his life miserable.'

A wave of applause began as the conductor came onto the podium. The houselights dimmed, and the evening of exquisite music began.

Alvirah, splendid in a dark-green velvet dinner gown, reached for Willy's hand.

An hour later, Sondra appeared onstage to tumultuous applause. Monsignor Ferris leaned over to whisper, 'As Willy would say, you did it again, Alvirah—and I'll never forget that you're the reason we have the bishop's chalice back. Too bad the diamond was lost, but the important thing is the chalice.'

'I think Willy deserves the credit,' Alvirah whispered in return. 'If his sheet music for "All Through the Night" hadn't been open on the piano, Sondra wouldn't have picked out the melody and sung it. That started me thinking; then when Stellina sang it in the pageant, I was sure.'

As Sondra raised her bow, they settled back

to listen. 'Look at that child,' Alvirah whispered to Willy, pointing to Stellina.

Clearly the little girl was transfixed by her mother's playing. Stellina's face shone with wonderment.

When the encore came, and Sondra began to play 'All Through the Night,' she looked up toward the box in which her daughter was seated. Audible only to those seated right around her, Stellina began to sing. No one could doubt that mother and daughter were performing to and for each other. For them, there was no one else in the world.

When the last notes died away, there was a hush. Then Willy leaned over and whispered, 'Alvirah, honey, it's too bad I didn't bring my sheet music. They could have used a little piano accompaniment. What do you think?'